Where to Find Dinosaurs Today

Where to Find
DINOSAURS
Today

Daniel and Susan Cohen

ILLUSTRATED WITH PHOTOGRAPHS

COBBLEHILL BOOKS

Dutton   New York

For photograph credits, see page 203.

Library of Congress Cataloging-in-Publication Data
Cohen, Daniel, date
Where to find Dinosaurs today / Daniel and Susan Cohen.
p.   cm.   Includes index.
ISBN 0-525-65098-9.—ISBN 0-14-036154-5
1. Dinosaurs—Catalogs and collections—United States.
2. Dinosaurs—Catalogs and collections—Canada.   I. Cohen,
Susan, date
II. Title.   QE862.D5C625   1992   567.9'1'0747—dc20
91-32084   CIP

Published in the United States 1992 by Cobblehill Books, an
affiliate of Dutton Children's Books, a division of Penguin Books
USA Inc., 375 Hudson Street, New York, New York 10014.
Published simultaneously in paperback 1992 by Puffin Books,
Penguin Books USA Inc.

Unicorn is a registered trademark of Dutton Children's Books

Designed by Mina Greenstein
Printed in the United States of America
First Edition   10   9   8   7   6   5   4   3   2   1

To *T. rex* and all the other creatures
of our dreams and nightmares

Contents

Introduction: Still Stalking the Earth   xi

Northeast

New York   3
Massachussets   12
Connecticut   18
Maine   23

Vermont   25
New Jersey   26
Pennsylvania   31

Southeast

Washington, D.C.   41
Maryland   44
Virginia   46
West Virginia   49
North Carolina   50
South Carolina   54
Georgia   55

Florida   57
Alabama   61
Louisiana   65
Mississippi   68
Arkansas   70
Tennessee   71

Midwest

Ohio   75
Kentucky   79
Indiana   82
Illinois   84
Michigan   89
Wisconsin   91

Minnesota   94
Iowa   95
Missouri   96
Kansas   99
Nebraska   102

Southwest

Texas   109
Oklahoma   117

New Mexico   119
Arizona   125

Rocky Mountains and Northern Great Plains

Colorado   131
Utah   136
Wyoming   146
South Dakota   149

North Dakota   155
Montana   156
Idaho   159

West Coast

California   163
Oregon   179

Washington   181

Alaska, Hawaii and Canada

Alaska   *185*   Canada   *188*
Hawaii   *187*

Photograph Credits   *203*

Index   *205*

Still Stalking
the Earth

The dinosaurs have been extinct for some sixty-five million years. The woolly mammoth and giant sloth have been dead for about ten thousand years. Yet all of these creatures can be seen in one form or another today, throughout the United States and Canada, and probably in greater numbers than at any time since they became extinct. This book will tell you where they can be found.

We have cast our net widely. There are listings from the very properly scientific to the frankly silly; from The Museum of Comparative Zoology at Harvard to a twice-life-size steel-and-concrete model of a *Brontosaurus* with a gift shop in its belly that stands near the Wheel Inn Restaurant on Interstate 10 at Cabazon, California.

Most of the listings are museums, fossil quarries, and "dinosaur parks," that is, places where models of dinosaurs and other prehistoric creatures have been set up. We have also listed places where you can buy dinosaurs or dinosaur motif merchandise. If money is no object, you can purchase a real *Triceratops* skull from Prehistoric Journeys. For those on a more modest budget, you can choose from over 120 different kinds of dinosaur T-shirts at Birmingham, Alabama's Dino-Store. There are also a few individuals worth meeting, like the world's greatest collector of dinosaur memorabilia (Dinosaur-abilia, he calls it), or the artist who creates marvelous dinosaur sculptures out of junked autos.

Just a quick aside on the use of the name *Brontosaurus*. We know that the proper scientific name for this gigantic sauropod is now *Apatosaurus*, but many of the places that we found still cling to *Brontosaurus*, sometimes for good historic reasons. If a particular set of bones in an exhibit was called *Brontosaurus* bones for a hundred years or more, a museum with a strong sense of its own history is reluctant to change the name. And if you stop by Flintstones Bedrock City in Custer, South Dakota, you are going to order a *bronto*burger, not an *apato*burger. Both names are used in this book, but *Brontosaurus* is preferred, for like the U.S. Postal Service, and at least some scientists, we have a fondness for the more familiar and widely accepted name.

The book is arranged by region, and then by state within the region. There are striking regional differences in what can be seen. Most (but not all) of the great museums are in the metropolitan areas of the Northeast. The most productive dinosaur fossil quarries are in the Northern Great Plains and Rocky Mountain states. There have been relatively few finds of dinosaurs in the Midwest, but Ice Age mammal fossils abound and are most frequently displayed. The best fossil elephant collection, for example, is at the University of Nebraska. Kansas was underwater during the Age of Dinosaurs, so few dinosaurs have been uncovered there, but there are lots of giant marine reptiles, every bit as fearsome-looking as the dinosaurs. As you might expect, California leads in the creation of dinosaur models. It is the home of the celebrated Dinamation robotic dinosaurs and other dinosaur robots which have been touring the country with such great success.

There are any number of ways this book can be used. Obviously, if the family is planning a trip to Mount Rushmore, you can remind them to stop off at Dinosaur Park, which is also in Rapid City, South Dakota, or at the nearby Mammoth Site. If you have to visit Aunt Edna and Uncle Jack in Pittsburgh and are wondering what to do with your free time, you will find that you can pay a visit to the original *Diplodocus* at the Carnegie Museum of Natural History. Just browsing through the entries you can learn things. For example, you will find out why the visually unimpressive fossils found near the little town of Parrsboro, Nova Scotia, in the 1980s have created so much excitement among scientists.

In putting together this book we naturally had to concentrate on the major museums and other sites—the American Museum of Natural History, Dinosaur National Park, the La Brea Tar Pits, and the like. But we took a particular delight in finding smaller, lesser-known or in some cases almost completely unknown, places. Everybody in Philadelphia knows about The Academy of Natural Sciences and its wonderful dinosaur collection. But practically no one has ever heard of the Wagner Free Institute of Science, a museum that has been virtually unchanged since it opened in the Victorian era. Here you can experience what it was like to go to a museum at a time when dinosaurs were first discovered, over a century ago.

We have listed lots of places, but we certainly haven't listed them all. There were some places where we couldn't get the needed information, and there undoubtedly are others that we just plain missed. If you know of anyplace that you think should be in this book, but isn't, contact us in care of the publishers, and we'll try to include it in a future edition.

The information in this book is as up-to-date as we could make it, but as the dinosaurs themselves would doubtless tell you (if they were able), things change. Hours and admission costs change frequently. If no admission charge is listed, the attraction is free. Attractions and even museums sometimes close. After trying to locate a dinosaur park in Wisconsin, we discovered it had been turned into a miniature golf course! A museum in Reno, Nevada, closed down. Most disruptive, however, are renovations. The great interest in dinosaurs, coupled with the enormous number of new discoveries over the past decade or so, plus advances in technology have made it necessary for many museums, including some of the biggest, to schedule major renovations of their paleontological collections. That's fine when the renovations are complete, but while they are going on, halls and entire exhibits can be closed, at least temporarily. Whenever possible, we have tried to give you some idea of what the renovation schedules might be. But we strongly suggest that if you plan to go out of your way to visit a particular museum or site, call ahead. We have provided the phone numbers.

A word of warning about fossils. Dinosaur and ancient mammal fossils are extremely rare and valuable to science. We have included a few places where fossil collecting is allowed, even encouraged. But the fossils are usually of the more common variety—shells and sharks' teeth. In the unlikely event that you come across a *Stegosaurus* rib, or mastodon tusk, don't touch it! Tell the local authorities what you have found. They will know what to do. In the past a lot of damage has been done to fossils by well-meaning, but inexperienced, collectors.

We can't tell you where you will be able to actually meet a living *Tyrannosaurus*, and you probably wouldn't want to anyway, but we can tell you where to find the closest thing to one.

DANIEL COHEN
SUSAN COHEN

NEW YORK

American Museum of Natural History

Where:	Central Park West at 79th Street, New York, NY 10024-5192
Hours:	10:00 A.M.-5:45 P.M. Sunday through Thursday; 10:00 A.M.-8:45 P.M. Friday and Saturday. Open every day except Thanksgiving and Christmas.
Admission:	Pay-what-you-wish admission policy, with $5 suggested for Adults, $2.50 for Children.
Phone:	(212) 769-5800

This famous New York City museum has the largest collection of dinosaur and other fossils of any museum in the world. Generations of New Yorkers and tourists have gaped in wonder and delight at the fearsome *Tyrannosaurus rex* skeleton, the *Brontosaurus*, the *Stegosaurus* and all the others in the fossil exhibits on the fourth floor. When you pictured a hall of dinosaurs in a museum, it was the Hall of Dinosaurs at the American Museum that first came to mind. Then, late in 1990, the American Museum announced that it was closing its dinosaur exhibit, and the rest of its fossil exhibits as well. But don't panic, the great museum is not being shut down permanently. The closings are necessary because the exhibits are going to be completely renovated and restructured. There have been no significant changes in these exhibits since the 1950s, and many are much older than that. For the visitor of the 1990s these closings can present a significant problem. Not all of the exhibits will be closed during the entire period of renovation. The whole project is scheduled to be completed late in 1995, and individual halls are not supposed to be closed for more than two years. But construction schedules, particularly for complicated and ambitious projects like this one, tend to slip and slide. So if you're planning to go to New York City and have your heart set on seeing the great dinosaurs at the American Museum, be sure to call ahead and find out what's open and what's closed. You may save yourself severe disappointment. However, there are plans for temporary exhibitions that show the work in progress during the construction period, and there will always be some sort of dinosaur exhibit on view.

The most spectacular new dinosaur display is not in the Hall of Dinosaurs at all. It was the first of the new exhibits to open, late in 1991. The exhibit dominates the cathedral-like Theodore Roosevelt Rotunda, the only place in the museum big enough to hold it. It shows an adult *Barosaurus*, a gigantic sauropod much like the *Brontosaurus*, attempting to defend its young against an attacking *Allosaurus*. The *Barosaurus* rears up on its hind legs and towers an incredible five stories, some 55 feet, above the visitors. This is, by far, the largest dinosaur fossil anywhere in the world and the first *Barosaurus* mounted in any museum. Some experts insist that the creature could never stand on its hind legs. The American Museum says it could, and intends to retain its reputation for exhibiting not only the best, and most, but the biggest. Actually the fossil is a cast of bones, because real fossil bones are far too heavy to be mounted in such a dramatic pose. Several real bones from the huge beast will be displayed elsewhere in the museum. Even if all of the other fossil exhibits are closed, this one makes a visit to the American Museum more than worthwhile.

The reconstructed fourth floor will have six individual halls, including two halls of dinosaurs, an orientation center, a hall focusing on fossil fish and amphibians, and two halls of fossil mammals. A main path in the form of an evolutionary tree will connect the six halls. Major events in evolutionary history will be featured on the main path, and placed in the context of Earth history. Branching from the main path, arranged

according to their evolutionary relationships, will be smaller paths exploring the diversity and adaptations within specific groups of animals.

Hundreds of specimens will be on view. Some of the old favorites will be displayed in more dramatic and accurate poses. Many new specimens will be exhibited. The famous *Tyrannosaurus rex* will be remounted so that its ferocious skull looms just above the heads of visitors.

New specimens will include the 15-million-year-old, bear-like carnivore, *Amphicyon*, shown at the moment it springs on its prey, the antelope-like *Ramoceros*.

The renovation will include new artwork and models, dramatic lighting, computer animation, interactive computer explanations, and possibly some dinosaur robots. The displays will also summarize some major scientific debates, such as the controversy over what caused the extinction of the dinosaurs.

The new fossil halls will be designed to appeal to visitors of all ages and levels of scientific sophistication. Information specifically for children will be presented; detailed information will be available for adults and for young museum visitors who are already dinosaur experts.

There has been some controversy over the planned renovations. There always is when changes are made in an institution as venerable and famous as the American Museum. One objection is that the dinosaurs will no longer be grouped chronologically but will instead be grouped according to shared physiological characteristics, even if they did not live at the same time or in the same place. Undoubtedly some long-time museum visitors will grumble that they liked it better before the renovations. But future generations of New Yorkers and visitors will gape in wonder and delight at these new displays, which will become as familiar and famous as the old ones were.

Dean Hannotte,
Dinosaurabilia Collector

Where: 151 First Avenue, New York, NY 10002
Phone: (212) 674-5848

"Dinosaur scholars visiting New York journey first to the Museum of Natural History, then speed down to E. 9th Street. There, in a cramped and cat fur-filled apartment, a genial man named Dean Hannotte introduces them to four friendly felines and one of the world's largest collections of dinosaurabilia—everything dinosauresque, except for (this is, after all, his *apartment*) skeletons." So wrote Lenore Skenazy in *The New York Daily News.*

Hannotte has been collecting dinosaur memorabilia since he was ten. Now his collection, which quite literally fills his

apartment from floor to ceiling, includes over 1,000 books, as well as films, records, newspaper stories, postcards, puzzles, and games with dinosaur themes. There are over 300 dinosaur toys, and a lot of advertising material from the old Sinclair Oil Company which used a *Brontosaurus* for its corporate symbol. "I'm more intrigued by man's fascination with the idea of prehistoric monsters than the actual creatures themselves," Hannotte explains.

Though an amateur, Hannotte is considered not only an expert but *the* expert in the field of Dinosaurabilia, and has lectured and served as a consultant to prestigious institutions like the American Museum of Natural History and The Academy of Natural Sciences in Philadelphia.

Hannotte loves to talk about his collection, and occasionally show it off. But remember, this is no museum open to the public, it's the man's apartment, so don't think you can just drop by. Call, or better still, write. You'll get an answer.

The New York State Museum

Where: Cultural Education Center of the Empire State Plaza, Albany, NY 12230
Hours: Museum open 10:00 A.M.-5:00 P.M. daily. Closed Thanksgiving, Christmas, and New Year's Day. Hours for the Dinosaur Discovery Center vary.
Phone: (518) 474-5877 or 474-5842

What started as a small experimental prototype called Dino Den proved to be so popular that it was expanded into a permanent exhibit, the Dinosaur Discovery Center. There are five different theme areas that cover such things as the size of dinosaurs and fossils. Each area has its own display, plus books, puzzles, and other objects. It's definitely a "hands-on" exhibit, where young visitors are encouraged to draw their own imaginary dinosaur or create dinosaur puppet performances. The Discovery Center is also used for various temporary displays, like robotic dinosaurs.

The museum has a permanent Ice Age exhibit, which includes a dandy model of a mother and baby mastodon. Once thought to have a thick coat of long, shaggy hair like its cousin, the mammoth, the mastodon is now known to have been covered with a finer, more delicate fur similar to that of a beaver or otter. This reconstruction is the first based on the new findings. By the way, The New York State Museum insists that this prehistoric pachyderm should properly be known as a mastodont. The "odont" refers to the animal's teeth. But since the final "t" is silent, the name is still pronounced "mastodon."

Louis Paul Jonas Studios, Inc.

Where: Box 193, RD 4, Hudson, NY 12534
Phone: (518) 851-2211

The artist Louis Paul Jonas was born in Budapest, Hungary, in 1894. When he came to the United States at the age of fourteen, he began working in a taxidermy shop owned by his brother, but he dreamed of doing more than stuffing hunting trophies. He spent a lot of time sketching and modeling animals. In 1915 the young man met Carl Akeley, the naturalist and artist who was preparing an enormous African elephant group for display in New York City's American Museum of Natural History. Jonas joined Akeley's staff as an apprentice. That launched him on a career of creating exhibits for museums. By 1940 he had established his own art studio to prepare animal models for museums and collectors. But Jonas, who had really started his career mounting elephants for museums, still wanted to do something bigger. He wanted to create dinosaurs.

In 1962 he got his chance when the Sinclair Oil Company commissioned his studio to fabricate nine authentic, full-size models of dinosaurs for the 1964–65 New York World's Fair. The company's trademark was the *Brontosaurus*. Forty-seven thousand pounds of clay were used in modeling the dinosaurs. The final products, cast in fiberglass and polyester resins, were the hit of the Fair. After the Fair closed, the nine original dinosaurs went on permanent display in different institutions throughout the country, and reproductions of the originals and other Jonas Studios dinosaurs can be found from Gastonia, South Carolina, to Edmonton, Alberta, and as far away as Australia. Jonas himself died in 1971, but Jonas Studios carries on his work. One-tenth scale models of a variety of dinosaurs, and models of other prehistoric animals like the woolly mammoth are available. These are not toys, but museum-quality replicas, and they cost a lot. *Tyrannosaurus* costs some $1,400, and *Brontosaurus* nearly twice as much. A much smaller *Coelophysis* goes for a mere $275. If that is in your price range, write to Jonas Studios for a complete list. Unfortunately, the studio does not have the staff to accommodate visitors.

Buffalo Museum of Science

Where: 1020 Humboldt Parkway, Buffalo, NY 14211-1293
Hours: 10:00 A.M.-5:00 P.M. seven days a week. Closed major
             holidays.
Admission: Adults $2.50; Children under 17 and Seniors $1.
Phone: (716) 896-5200

The hall called Dinosaurs and Co. contains a fine collection of well-displayed fossils. The pride of the collection is undoubtedly the complete and original *Allosaurus* skeleton. There is also a complete *Triceratops* skeleton; it's a cast, but the average visitor will never know the difference. There are dinosaur eggs, teeth, even a fossil impression of dinosaur skin. In the "and Co." part of the exhibit there are a variety of fossils of marine reptiles—a mosasaur skull and flying reptiles like the pterosaurs. But where this museum really excels is in its collection of early mammals. In addition to the familiar saber-toothed cat and primitive whale, there is the oldest known complete bat fossil. It's not impressive to look at, but scientifically it is very important, because bat fossils are rare, and most museums don't show them. There is also a complete cast of Lucy, the famous early humanlike creature and possibly our own direct ancestor.

The Museum of Comparative Zoology

Where: On the campus of Harvard University, Cambridge, MA 02138

Hours: Monday through Friday, 9:00 A.M.-4:30 P.M.; Sunday, 1:00 P.M.-4:30 P.M. Closed Christmas, New Year's Day, 4th of July.

Admission: Adults $3; Seniors and Students $2; Children $1.

Phone: (619) 495-2463

Alfred S. Romer was, for many years, one of the world's leading paleontologists, and for over fifteen years he was head of this Harvard museum. The great hall of vertebrate paleontology is named in his honor. The collection here is both astonishing, and historically important. The visitor will not find robotic dinosaurs, computer animation, or any of the other trendy features of modern museum display. This is an old-fashioned museum with glass cases and long written explanations of what's in them. But it has an absolutely marvelous collection. Don't just rush from one big skeleton to the other; get a gallery guide, which will tell you not only what you are looking at but where it came from, and why it's important. This museum demands and deserves the visitor's attention and time.

As soon as you enter the hall you will see an enormous turtle shell. It's 7 feet 2 inches long and comes from an animal called *Stupendemys*, which means "astonishing turtle." It is not only astonishing, it is the largest turtle ever discovered. It lived five or six million years ago in the wet lowlands of South America.

Fossil fishes don't normally attract a lot of casual attention, but among the fossils is a preserved specimen of *Latimeria chalumnae*, a species of coelacanth. This is a type of fish that lived in the time of the dinosaurs, and which scientists had believed was extinct for as long as the dinosaurs. At least they believed that until 1938 when one of them was caught very much alive, off the coast of South Africa. Since then nearly a hundred have been caught and identified. The Harvard specimen was caught in 1965. They have changed little over millions of years, and can be considered true living fossils.

Dimetrodon, a fierce-looking creature with powerful jaws and an enormous "sail" on its back, is often mistaken for a dinosaur, but it isn't even a close relative. The museum has an excellent specimen and the creature has been adopted as the institution's symbol.

Among the dinosaur fossils, the main attraction surely must be the *Triceratops* skull found in Wyoming in 1930. This is not only a *Triceratops* fossil, it is THE *Triceratops* fossil, the type for this species of dinosaur. All newly discovered fossils must match this one if they are to be given the same name.

More impressive than any single dinosaur in the Harvard collection is a 42-foot specimen of *Kronosaurus*, a fierce-looking marine reptile from the Age of Dinosaurs. The fossil was discovered in Australia in 1931, and lay around in the museum basement for years because there wasn't enough money to finish the task of mounting it. Then Romer met the wealthy Boston manufacturer Godfrey Lowell Cabot, a man fascinated by stories of sea serpents. His great-grandfather had reported seeing one in Gloucester Harbor, and the story became part of family lore. Romer told him about the skeleton in the basement that looked like a sea serpent. Cabot asked how much restoration would cost. Romer guessed about $10,000. Cabot immediately sent a check, and in 1958 this enormous and frightening fossil was put on display.

The museum also has an impressive collection of prehistoric mammals, including the first complete mastodon skeleton ever exhibited anywhere. The original plaques listing the citizens of Boston and Cambridge who put up the money to buy the skeleton and donate it to Harvard are still in the case with the mastodon.

In this museum the visitor not only learns about the history of life on Earth, but about the history of the discovery of ancient life as well.

Museum of Science

Where: Science Park, Boston, MA 02114-1099
Hours: Tuesday through Sunday, 9:00 A.M.-5:00 P.M. Open until 9:00 P.M. Friday nights. Closed most Mondays and major holidays.
Admission: Varies, depending on shows or events the visitor wishes to attend.
Phone: General information (617) 723-2500; Recorded information (617) 742-6088

Traveling exhibits, a planetarium, and a state-of-the-art theater with a wraparound screen and 84 loudspeakers are the most notable features of this popular Boston institution. Robotic dinosaurs have made several appearances here. But there are also permanent exhibits, including a full-size *Tyrannosaurus rex* model and a number of fossil casts. Call to find out what special events are coming up.

Springfield Science Museum

Where: 236 State Street, Springfield, MA 01103. Located just off Route 1-91.

Hours: Tuesday through Sunday, noon-5:00 P.M.; Closed Mondays and major holidays.

Admission: Suggested donation: Adults $2; Children $1.

Phone: (413) 733-1194

The pride of this museum's Dinosaur Hall is a full-sized *Tyrannosaurus rex* model. There is also a *Stegosaurus* skeleton and a model of *Coelophysis*, a dinosaur that once lived in the Springfield area. The museum, which tries to have as many "hands-on" exhibits as possible, has a dinosaur leg bone, some fossil tracks, and a variety of other fossils that visitors can reach out and touch. There is much else earthly (live snakes) to unearthly (a planetarium) to be found in the museum.

Pratt Museum of Natural History

Where: The campus of Amherst College, Amherst, MA 01002

Hours: Open during the academic year Monday through Friday, 9:00 A.M.-3:30 P.M.; Saturday, 10:00 A.M.-4:00 P.M.; Sunday, noon-5:00 P.M.

Phone: (413) 542-2165

In 1802 a New England farm boy named Pliny Moody found fossil tracks in sandstones exposed near his home in South Hadley, Massachusetts. These footprints looked as if they had been made by gigantic birds, and were regarded by most people as the fossil footprints of huge ground-living birds. Within the next two or three decades many more of these "bird tracks" were found up and down the length of the Connecticut River

Valley. The tracks fascinated the Reverend E.B. Hitchcock, president of Amherst College. He collected as many of them as he could and his collection formed the basis for the fossil exhibits in the college's natural history museum.

There is a lot more than fossil dinosaur tracks in this excellent museum. As soon as you enter, you see a platform with the skeletons of a mastodon, mammoth, Irish elk, saber-toothed cat, and dire wolf. A couple of more unusual specimens are a cave bear, not often shown in American museums, and a moa, a huge flightless bird which, until fairly recent times, survived in New Zealand. Among the dinosaur fossils are a *Kritosaurus*, one of the duck-billed dinosaurs, a skull of *Triceratops*, and a cast of a *Tyrannosaurus* skull. While looking at the displays be sure not to overlook the two skulls and skeleton of the large amphibian called *Eryops*. This flat-headed animal was among the earliest vertebrates adapted for extensive walking on the land.

When you have finished your visit to the museum, you can stroll around the Amherst campus.

Nash Dinosaurland

Where: Off Route 116 in South Hadley, MA 01075 near the Granby town line.
Hours: Daily 8:30 A.M.-5:00 P.M., from April 1 to Christmas.
Admission: 50¢
Phone: (413) 467-9566

Dinosaur tracks have been found in many parts of the Northeast, but back in the 1930s not a great deal of attention was paid to them by the general public. However, Carleton Nash, whose family was among the first settlers in the Hadley area, had studied geology at nearby Amherst College, and thought he saw a unique business opportunity. The owner of the land rich in tracks was about to dynamite the footprint-bearing rocks for building stone. Nash bought the land and opened what he calls the "world's largest dinosaur footprint quarry."

Dinosaurland, which has now been in operation for half a century, is part-quarry, part-souvenir shop, and part-Carleton Nash. The shop displays, and sells, tracks and a variety of other fossils. The tracks run from $25 to several hundred dollars, depending on size and quality. In addition, there are plastic dinosaur models and a miscellaneous collection of other items. The tracks can be used as stepping-stones in garden walks, as plaques, paperweights, even ashtrays. The quarry itself, in back of the shop, is not really open to the public, though Nash has been known to show it to visitors. Nash himself is something of a character who is not at all adverse to chatting about his finds and some of the famous people who have purchased them over the last half century. This place is one of a kind and definitely worth a visit if you are in the vicinity. If you can't get there, you can write or call for information about what's for sale.

CONNECTICUT

The Peabody Museum

Where: On the campus of Yale University, 170 Whitney Avenue, corner of Whitney Avenue and Sachem Street, New Haven, CT 06511

Hours: Monday through Saturday, 9:00 A.M.-4:45 P.M.; Sundays and holidays, 1:00 P.M.-4:45 P.M. Closed New Year's Day, 4th of July, Thanksgiving, and Christmas.

Admission: Adults $2; Seniors $1.50; Children 5 to 15 years $1, under 5 years free.

Phone: Info tape (203) 432-5050; Events tape (203) 432-5799; Main number (203) 432-3775

In many ways Yale's Peabody Museum can be called "the house that dinosaurs built." Pioneer American paleontologist Othniel Charles Marsh persuaded his fabulously wealthy uncle, George Peabody, to donate $150,000 to establish a natural history museum at Yale. That was big money back in 1866. The original museum building was opened to the public in 1876. O.C. Marsh was its first curator of paleontology and anthropology.

At the time, Marsh was engaged in a bitter rivalry with his hated foe, Philadelphia's Edward Drinker Cope, over who was to be America's, and perhaps the world's, top paleontologist. The dispute has been called "The Great Fossil Feud" or "Dinosaur Wars," for much of it was fought over who was to have access to the enormous finds of giant dinosaurs that were then being made in the American West. Marsh, having the deeper pockets, got the better specimens and most of them went right to the Peabody, which quickly amassed one of the best dinosaur fossil collections in the world.

The first *Brontosaurus* skeleton to be mounted—all 67 feet

18

of it—was collected by Marsh and put on display at the Peabody. It still dominates the Great Hall of Dinosaurs. Never mind that the proper name for the creature is now *Apatosaurus*, Marsh called it a *Brontosaurus*, and at the Peabody it's *still* a *Brontosaurus*. It does, however, have a new head. For over a century this display had the wrong head, and a plaque near the old head explains how the mistake was made. Also on display in the Great Hall is the first full *Stegosaurus* skeleton ever mounted and skeletons of *Camptosaurus, Anatosaurus,* skulls from horned dinosaurs, and a cast of a skull of the famed *Tyrannosaurus rex.*

The Peabody, however, is not only a showplace for dinosaur fossils discovered in the nineteenth century. In 1988 the museum unveiled a display of *Deinonychus,* or "Terrible Claw," one of the most significant finds of recent years. *Deinonychus* lived 100 million years ago, and its remains were first found in Montana in 1964 by an expedition led by Yale's John H. Ostrom. Though *Deinonychus* was small for a dinosaur, approximately 150 pounds and almost five feet tall, it was an unusually active and agile carnivorous creature. Its most distinguishing feature was a large sickle-shaped claw on each of its hind feet, from which Professor Ostrom coined its name. The *Deinonychus* discovery led Ostrom to theorize that this dinosaur and others may have been warm-blooded. Ostrom also reintroduced the theory that birds are the most logical descendants of the dinosaurs.

The *Deinonychus* exhibit includes a full-sized, fleshed-out, color model of the dinosaur and two mounted skeletons that are exact replicas of the original fossil material: one in an attacking pose, the other in a striding posture. These represent a major departure from the static fossil reconstructions of earlier eras.

The most impressive fossil in the Great Hall, however, is not a dinosaur at all, but a skeleton of *Archelon ischyros,* a gigantic turtle that lived over 100 million years ago.

On a wall of the Great Hall is the 110-foot-long, Pulitzer Prize-winning mural, "The Age of Reptiles," by Rudolph Zallinger. There is some question as to whether dinosaurs were really reptiles, and the reconstructions in the mural may be a bit dated but, never mind, it will still knock your eyes out.

The Hall of Prehistoric Mammals has another Zallinger mural, called, naturally, "The Age of Mammals."

You can purchase all sorts of modestly priced dinosaur trinkets at a children's shop called, inevitably, the DinoStore. It is attached to the regular Museum Shop, which sells a wider variety of higher-priced items. Specialties are *Deinonychus* or *Archelon* sweat shirts, and giant-sized color posters of the Zallinger murals.

The museum hosts a variety of dinosaur-related events throughout the year, including a *Brontosaurus* Concert, a midday musical performance held in the Great Hall of Dinosaurs, and Dinosaur Days, a week-long celebration of the dinosaur collection. Phone to find out the time of special events.

In nice weather, you can picnic on the hill behind the neo-Gothic structure, and stroll the beautiful Yale campus.

Dinosaur State Park

Where: West Street, a half mile east of Interstate 91 (Exit 23) in Rocky Hill, CT.

Hours: Park: Daily 9:00 A.M.-4:30 P.M. Exhibit Center: Tuesday through Sunday 9:00 A.M.-4:30 P.M. Closed Mondays, New Year's Day, Thanksgiving, and Christmas.

Admission: There is a small fee.

Phone: (203) 529-8423

One hundred and eighty-five million years ago, in the early part of the Jurassic Period, dinosaurs tromped across the mudflats of what is now the Connecticut Valley. They left behind their footprints. Because of a unique set of circumstances, some of these footprints were preserved in the sandstones, siltstones, and mudstones of the Valley.

The tracks were uncovered in 1966 by a bulldozer operator clearing land for a new state building. The first excavation exposed nearly 1,500 tracks. Later excavations located hundreds more. It is the largest dinosaur trackway ever found in North America.

The fossil tracks are three-toed impressions ranging from ten to sixteen inches in length. No one is sure which specific dinosaur made the tracks. The size of the footprints and the four-foot pace indicate that the adult animals were about 8 feet tall and 20 feet long. The best guess is that the trackmaker was *Dilophosaurus*, a carnivorous dinosaur, or something very like it.

The majority of the tracks were reburied for preservation, but several hundred are on display within a geodesic dome which serves as the park's Exhibit Center. The trackway is dramatically lighted, and impressive to see. You can actually follow some of the individual trails. In addition to the tracks themselves, there is a full-size reconstruction of *Dilophosaurus*, examples of different kinds of fossil dinosaur tracks, and other dinosaur-related material. But it is the trackway itself that is the big attraction here.

The Exhibit Center contains an auditorium, a discovery room, and a small bookstore and gift shop. The volunteer staff is exceptionally knowledgeable and helpful.

Outside there are nature trails and a picnic area. For the serious dinosaur buff there is a place where you can make casts of real dinosaur footprints. The service is free but you have to supply your own materials, ten to fifteen pounds of plaster of Paris and some cooking oil.

Every year the park holds a popular Dinomania Festival. Collectors of dinosaur memorabilia, anything from books to Flintstone figures, come to display their wares for sale and swap. Call the park for dates and other details.

The Children's Museum
of Maine

Where: On the campus of Westbrook College, 746 Stevens Avenue, Portland, ME 04103

Hours: 9:30 A.M.-4:30 P.M. seven days a week. Closed major holidays.

Admission: Everyone over the age of one and under the age of 65 pays $2.50. Admission for Seniors is $2. Half price for everyone on Wednesday afternoons during the school year.

Phone: (207) 797-5483

Designed as a "hands-on" museum for younger children, there are exhibits on computers, TV, railroading and, on the third floor, the Dino Den. Here visitors can see dinosaur tracks, replicas of dinosaur eggs, real fossils, a wooden *Stegosaurus* skeleton, and a diorama of prehistoric life. There is a cave to crawl in, fossils to touch, and a box of sand where youngsters can dig for replicas of saber-toothed cat claws and sharks' teeth.

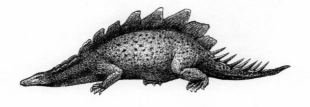

Maine State Museum

Where: State Capitol Complex, State House Station 83, Augusta, ME 04333
Hours: Monday through Friday, 9:00 A.M.-5:00 P.M.; Saturday, 10:00 A.M.-4:00 P.M.; Sunday, 1:00 P.M.-4:00 P.M. Closed New Year's Day, Thanksgiving, and Christmas.
Phone: (207) 289-2301

This museum concentrates on Maine's historical past, but a new Ice Age exhibit gives visitors a glimpse into the prehistoric past. No dinosaur fossils have been found in the state, but there have been mammoth and mastodon remains, some of which are on display, and there is a fossil walrus skull found by a bulldozer operator digging the foundation for a radar station.

VERMONT

Fairbanks Museum and Planetarium

Where: St. Johnsburg, VT
Hours: Monday through Saturday, 10:00 A.M.-4:00 P.M., until
           6:00 P.M. during July and August. Sunday, 1:00 P.M.-
           5:00 P.M.
Admission: Adults $3; Children $2.
Phone: (802) 748-2372

The planetarium is the major attraction at this institution. But while going to gaze at the stars, be sure not to overlook a glimpse into the past. There is a nice display of fossil material and casts. There is, for example, a good cast of a small *Plesiosaurus* and some original mammoth and mastodon teeth. An especially interesting item is a small dinosaur fossil only partially removed from its surrounding matrix. This graphically shows what fossils look like when they are found, and how they are prepared.

New Jersey State Museum

Where: 205 West State Street, Trenton, NJ 08625-0530
Hours: Tuesday through Saturday, 9:00 A.M.-4:45 P.M.; Sunday, noon-5:00 P.M. Closed Mondays and state holidays.
Phone: Recorded message about current activities (609) 292-6464; Additional information (609) 292-6308

The Hall of Nature on the second floor has exhibits explaining how the Earth began, and the sort of creatures that lived long ago, particularly in the New Jersey area. There is, for example, the nearly complete skeleton of a hadrosaur, or duck-billed dinosaur, discovered in the town of Haddonfield, New Jersey, in 1858. Mastodon bones are available for touching. In addition to its exhibits, the museum runs a wide variety of programs for children, the most popular called Dino-Safari, which uses slides, films, and actual fossils from the museum's large collection. The program is repeated several times during February and March, and advance reservations are required. When the weather warms up the museum sponsors fossil-collecting trips. Call for details.

Jim Gary's Twentieth-Century Dinosaurs

Where: 35-B Hollywood Avenue, Farmingdale, NJ 07727
Phone: (201) 938-6281

Artist Jim Gary turns junk auto parts and other discards of modern civilization into amusing and astonishing dinosaur sculptures. Up until the mid-1970s Gary had been a fairly

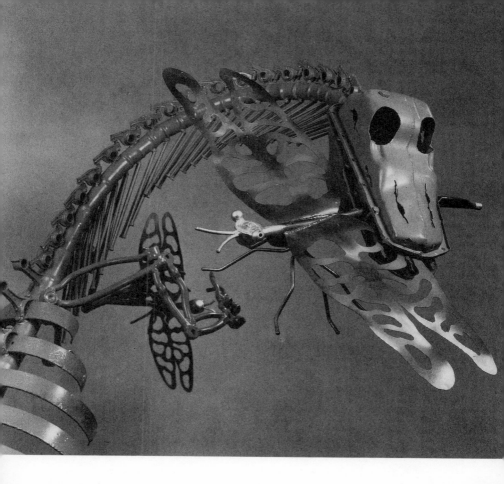

conventional metal sculptor. Then one day while visiting a scrapyard looking for interesting pieces of metal to be used in his sculpture, the self-taught artist began thinking of the scrapyard as a burial ground for the remains of twentieth-century technology. He imagined future scientists studying the remains of junked automobiles in much the same way as today's scientists study fossils from the Age of Dinosaurs. From there it was only a short mental step—combined, of course, with years of hard work—to produce the first of his now celebrated Twentieth-Century Dinosaurs.

Gary's creations are large, though not necessarily life-size. One of his biggest, the *Brontosaurus* (or *Apatosaurus*), is 42 feet long, whereas the real thing might reach 80 feet. Each sculpture takes parts from about a dozen cars, and six-to-eight months of cutting and welding to complete. The artist uses many different parts of the cars—leaf springs, oil pans, radius rods, and just about anything else. He used the top of an old Volkswagen Beetle for the shell of a giant turtle. Gary says that he tries to get parts from the older cars because, "The new cars are not decent material." When the piece is finished it is painted, usually in vivid colors. The result is a creation that is imaginative and yet surprisingly lifelike. His *Tyrannosaurus* looks as if it is about to attack.

It took a few years for Gary's creations to be recognized. His first major show was at the Philadelphia Academy of Natural Sciences, a natural history museum, not an art museum. That was in 1979, and since then his career has blossomed. His creations have now been shown all over the United States and as far away as Australia and Japan. In 1990 two dozen of Gary's metal monsters were displayed to enthusiastic crowds at the Smithsonian Institution in Washington, D.C. He has been written up in everything from *Ranger Rick* to *Motor Trend*, and has appeared frequently on television. If a traveling show of Gary's dinosaurs comes to your area, don't miss it!

Gary sells his creations, and he still recalls how one woman wanted the dinosaur set up in her living room. But the size of these creatures and the price (between $50,000 and $100,000) make them prohibitive for the average family living room.

The artist has kept about thirty of his favorite pieces, and ultimately hopes to turn the area around his studio into a sculpture park. If you phone, or preferably write, you might be able to arrange a visit. But remember, this man is an artist not a museum guide, and he spends most of his time working, or on the road with his traveling exhibits. Some of his dinosaurs are also on public display in front of the Jones Lane Elementary School in Rockville, Maryland. For information contact Montgomery County Public Schools, 850 Hungerford Drive, Rockville, Maryland 20850, phone (301) 279-3391.

Rutgers Geology Museum

Where: Geology building on the College Avenue campus of Rutgers University, New Brunswick, NJ 08903
Hours: Monday, 1:00 P.M.-4:00 P.M.; Tuesday through Friday, 9:00 A.M.-noon.
Phone: (201) 932-7243

This museum concentrates on fossils found in New Jersey. The best dinosaur material on display are dinosaur tracks, which have been found in abundance in the state. There is also an excellent mastodon exhibit. The skeleton on exhibit was found in Salem County, New Jersey, in 1870. The farmer who found it sold it to a circus, and the museum purchased it a couple of years later. The skeleton was first mounted in 1896 and remounted in 1932. It is fairly complete by mastodon standards. Only the legs and tusks have been reconstructed.

Princeton Natural History Museum

Where: Guyot Hall, on Washington Street on the campus of Princeton University, Princeton, NJ
Hours: Generally 9:00 A.M.-5:00 P.M. on days when other university buildings are open, but it's best to check.
Phone: Central number (609) 258-3000. Museum number (609) 258-1322.

This university museum has a tiny staff, and is not really equipped to handle crowds of visitors. But it does have some things worth seeing, including a fully mounted *Allosaurus*, a replica of baby dinosaurs found in a nest in Montana, and a couple of dandy Irish elk skeletons.

The Morris Museum

Where: 6 Normandy Heights Road, Morristown, NJ 07960
Hours: Monday through Saturday, 10:00 A.M.-5:00 P.M.; Sunday, 1:00 P.M.-5:00 P.M. Closed on major holidays.
Admission: Adults $2; Children, Students, and Seniors $1.
Phone: (201) 538-0454

This is an extremely pleasant and apparently well-funded local museum. The collection contains everything from contemporary paintings to a mini-zoo. For a museum of its size, it has a fine dinosaur display. Pride of the museum are the dinosaur tracks, many of which come from New Jersey. However, the visitor is likely to be struck first by a large model of a *Pteranodon* suspended from the ceiling and the nearly full-size *Stegosaurus* up against the wall. The museum is undergoing renovations and its fossil exhibits will be expanded.

PENNSYLVANIA

The Academy of Natural Sciences

Where: 19th Street and the Parkway, Philadelphia, PA 19103
Hours: Monday through Friday, 10:00 A.M.-4:30 P.M.; Saturday, Sunday, holidays, 10:00 A.M.-5:00 P.M. Closed Thanksgiving, Christmas, and New Year's Day.
Admission: Adults $5.50; Seniors and Military $5; Children 3 to 12 years $4.50, under 3 years free.
Phone: (215) 299-1020

The Academy, founded in 1912, is arguably the oldest institution devoted to natural science in America. But there is nothing old-fashioned about its dinosaur exhibit. The exhibit was completely revamped in the late 1980s to encompass all of the latest theories about dinosaurs and all of the latest techniques for making the display informative and exciting to the public. The result is one of the very best dinosaur exhibits that has ever been created. Though there are excellent displays of modern animals (some living, as in a zoo, many stuffed), Egyptian mummies, gems and crystals, and other items of interest, it is the dinosaurs that are the Academy stars and the dinosaurs that bring in the crowds. You know that when you walk up to the front door, for you are greeted by a striking bronze sculpture of a pair of the swift and agile dinosaurs, *Deinonychus*.

Suspended over the lobby where you buy your ticket is a 40-foot *Elasmosaurus* skeleton. Turn right and you are in the exhibit called Discovering Dinosaurs. The first thing that commands the visitor's attention is the huge *Tyrannosaurus rex* skeleton. During the renovations the posture of the creature was completely changed to reflect the new scientific view of

dinosaurs. It is no longer a clumsy tail-dragging sluggard. *T. rex* leans forward, with its tail held out stiffly behind, in a sleek running posture. The historic *Hadrosaurus* or duck-billed dinosaur skeleton, the first dinosaur skeleton unearthed in the Western Hemisphere, has also been dramatically rearranged. Overhead a *Pteranodon* spreads its enormous wings.

No complete skeleton of *Ultrasaurus* has been found yet, but enough has been discovered to make scientists believe that this creature is the largest known dinosaur. There is a replica of the front leg of this giant; it's 20 feet high. You don't really know how big that is until you stand next to it and imagine what the rest of the beast would have looked like!

While the elegant and impressive skeletons are clearly the focal point of Discovering Dinosaurs, there are also a variety of interpretative exhibitions which examine such questions as were the dinosaurs warm-blooded and why did they become extinct? A small theater provides a multimedia show on the history of the scientific discovery of dinosaurs. Next to it is a striking re-creation of a habitat from the Late Cretaceous Period (the final stage of the Age of Dinosaurs). The re-creation features both the lifelike model of a small dinosaur, and a living opossum, whose direct ancestors shared the world with dinosaurs.

While the science is all up-to-date, the Academy has found space for a little dinosaur fun as well. There is a dandy display of Dinosaurabilia, and a really entertaining video show called "Dinos in the Movies." A fine display of dinosaur art graces the walls of the exhibit.

The Academy hosts occasional traveling exhibits like the robotic dinosaurs, but it is the permanent exhibit that should not be missed.

The Academy is located in the middle of Philadelphia's museum row, with art museums, technology museums, and other fine attractions within easy walking distance.

Wagner Free Institute
of Science

Where: Montgomery Avenue and 17th Street, Philadelphia, PA
19121
Hours: Tuesday to Friday 10:00 A.M.-4:00 P.M. by appointment.
Closed Mondays and legal holidays.
Phone: (215) 763-6529

Stepping into the Wagner Free Institute is like stepping into a time warp. Suddenly you are back in the middle of the last century, the Victorian era, when men wore high silk hats or derbies. Under the seats of the Institute's lecture hall are metal racks to hold these hats. The exhibits are identified by hand-written labels, many over 100 years old. The collection contains everything from dinosaur bones to cases full of neatly pinned butterflies and moths to Indian artifacts, all displayed in a long, high-ceilinged gallery lighted by 25-foot-tall windows. It is the most perfectly preserved Victorian-era museum in America, perhaps in the world, and is already on the National Register of Historic Places and heading for designation as a National Historic Landmark. This is truly a museum's museum.

The Wagner Institute in its present location was first opened to the general public in 1865. It was the creation of William Wagner, a wealthy Philadelphia merchant and an enthusiastic amateur scientist, a collector of fossils and other natural history specimens who wanted to provide a place where ordinary people could learn about science. Access to the collections and the lectures was free then, and is free now.

For years the Wagner Institute was a leading force in scientific education in Philadelphia, and was well known by the scientifically minded throughout the country. But slowly its reputation began to fade. Wagner, and the trustees who directed the Institute after his death (usually Wagner family

members), were fiercely devoted to keeping the Institute in-
dependent. Wagner's devotion to the Institute he had created
may be gauged by the fact that he was buried in a crypt in the
basement, though after a year or so his widow had the remains
removed to a more conventional burial place. The founder
had left his creation with enough of an endowment to keep it
running, but there was not enough money for great expansion.
So the Wagner Institute remained essentially unchanged in
the midst of a changing world. The area around the Institute
has changed most dramatically. Originally it was a parklike
suburban location; now the building is in the middle of a
crumbling urban ghetto, surrounded by decaying and aban-
doned row houses. This once-thriving institution was virtually
forgotten. People who taught the history of science at the
University of Pennsylvania didn't even know it still existed.

But the benign neglect has turned out to be a blessing in
disguise, for while other Victorian-era museums have been
either modernized, absorbed, or disbanded, the Wagner Institute has remained perfectly preserved, like many of the fossils
on display in its glass cases. And now the Wagner Institute
has been rediscovered, and is experiencing a modest renais-
sance. In October, 1990, the historic lecture hall was the site
of a two-day dinosaur symposium, at which many of the country's leading dinosaur experts spoke. The scientists, most of
whom had never been to the Institute before, indeed had never
heard of it, were amazed and charmed at delivering a talk from
behind the same lectern used a century ago by Edward Drinker
Cope and other great paleontologists of that era.

Articles in Philadelphia newspapers increased the number
of visitors, though any potential visitor is strongly encouraged
to call ahead for an appointment, for the Institute's tiny staff
can only cope with a limited number of people at any given
time. And since many of the exhibits are old, fragile, and very
easy to reach, all children must be accompanied by an adult.
There are also renovations going on, though staff members

are quick to say that the work is strictly for preservation, that nothing is going to be changed. After a century or so, a little repair work is needed.

What will the visitor see at the Wagner Institute? One of the prizes of the collection are *Brontosaurus* bones collected by Cope, and displayed in the gallery under his direction. There is no thought of calling them *Apatosaurus* bones at the Wagner. These bones appear exactly as they did when they were taken from the ground in Colorado. They have not been painted brown like most dinosaur bones shown in modern museums. There are other fossils of historic significance as well. But most of all, the visitor sees and feels what a museum was like a century or more ago. That is an experience you can't get anywhere else.

The Carnegie Museum of Natural History

Where: 440 Forbes Avenue, Pittsburgh, PA 15213
Hours: Tuesday through Saturday, 10:00 A.M.-5:00 P.M.; open Friday until 1:00 P.M.; Sunday, 1:00 P.M.-5:00 P.M.
Phone: (412) 622-3172

The justly celebrated Dinosaur Hall of the Carnegie Museum contains one of the very best collections of dinosaur fossils in the world. There are the full skeletons of eleven different and mostly spectacular species on display here. The specimens are arranged in chronological order, starting with the carnivorous *Allosaurus* and a *Stegosaurus*.

Next comes *Diplodocus*, the longest animal known to have ever walked the earth. This particular skeleton extends 78 feet, but six feet of its tail were removed. The creature has a particular significance to this museum because the steel magnate Andrew Carnegie, who founded the institution and after whom it is named, financed the expedition that first found *Diplodocus* and brought the skeleton to Pittsburgh. Scientists named the new species of dinosaur *Diplodocus carnegii* in his honor. Carnegie became interested in dinosaurs in 1898 when he read a newspaper article on dinosaur finds in Wyoming. The *Diplodocus* skeleton was put on exhibit in 1907 after the building was expanded to provide a large enough hall to hold the enormous creature.

Next to *Diplodocus* is the other giant plant eater, *Brontosaurus* (or *Apatosaurus*). Dominating the far end of the hall is *Tyrannosaurus rex*, who stands about 20 feet tall. And there are other full and partial skeletons as well.

Most of the skeletons on exhibit were found by Carnegie scientists between 1902 and 1923, and have been on display since the 1940s. But in recent years new excavations have produced a flood of new fossil material. The museum collection now contains approximately 500 dinosaur specimens (mostly single bones). Many of the newer specimens are for study only or are being prepared in basement workrooms for future display.

Though dinosaurs are by far the most impressive fossils in this museum, there are many others worth seeing. There are, for example, several excellent pterosaur specimens, and many of the best known Ice Age mammals—saber-toothed cats, mammoths, mastodons, and the elaborately antlered Irish elk.

Southeast

WASHINGTON D.C.

National Museum of
Natural History
Smithsonian Institution

Where: Tenth Street and Constitution Avenue N.W., Wash-
              ington, DC. On the National Mall between the Wash-
              ington Monument and the Capitol.
Hours: Open daily except Christmas Day, 10:00 A.M.-5:30 P.M.
              Hours are usually extended during the spring and
              summer.
Admission: Free, except for occasional special exhibits.
Phone: (202) 357-2700

There are nine different Smithsonian museums located on the
National Mall. You can recognize the National Museum of
Natural History immediately because Uncle Beazley is stand-
ing in front. Uncle Beazley is a life-sized fiberglass model of
Triceratops, and a big favorite of young visitors, who like to
be photographed standing alongside him.

Fossils are displayed in a series of halls called The History
of Life, which take the visitor from the earliest fossils through
the Ice Age. *Tyrannosaurus*, *Stegosaurus*, and other well-
known dinosaurs are represented in this excellent collection.
The undoubted star is a full-scale skeleton of *Diplodocus*, the
longest-known dinosaur. Hovering overhead is a huge pterosaur model.

Usually the preparation of fossils is an activity that goes on
in a museum's basement or back rooms, and well out of public
view. But at the National Museum of Natural History much
of this work goes on behind a glass wall in full view of visitors.
It is one of the three public viewing paleontological laboratories
in the country. You can actually watch scientists at the precise

and painstaking work of extracting delicate fossils from rocks, and reconstructing models from partial skeletons.

The latest, and last, of the museum's complex of paleontological exhibits is Life in the Ancient Seas, which opened in May, 1990. This exhibit traces life in the sea, and shimmering lighting gives the visitor the feeling of actually being underwater. Models of huge fish, giant squid, and other sea creatures are suspended overhead, and two enormous murals depict life-size prehistoric creatures swimming underwater. The largest mural, measuring 16 feet high by 120 feet long, features a 20-foot-long mosasaur (marine lizard) and a 45-foot-long *Basilosaurus* (ancient whale). Either of these creatures could have served as the model for the legendary sea serpent. Fossil skeletons of these and other creatures are on display in front of the murals.

If you like big, though not necessarily ancient, animals, another hall contains a full-scale model of the blue whale, the largest creature that has ever lived. There is also an insect zoo, where the exhibits are small, but still alive. This is just a sampling of the delights that can be found in this truly national museum. Be sure to leave plenty of time in your schedule to see the museum because there is so much to see. And check the museum calendar, because there are lots of free films, lectures, and other special events.

Calvert Marine Museum

Where: On Route 2 in Solomons, Calvert County, southern Maryland, twenty miles south of Prince Frederick. The museum is on Back Creek, two nautical miles from Chesapeake Bay, and can also be reached by boat. Museum dock facilities are free to visitors.

Hours: May through September, 10:00 A.M.-5:00 P.M. daily; October through April, 10:00 A.M.-4:30 P.M. Monday through Friday; noon to 4:30 P.M. Saturday and Sunday. Closed New Year's Day, Thanksgiving, and Christmas.

Phone: (301) 326-2042

The Calvert Marine Museum was established in 1970, primarily to house artifacts of the region's rich fishing and boat-building history. However, the museum has always displayed fossils found in the area and in recent years this display has expanded enormously. A newly opened fossil hall takes visitors through a re-creation of the sea that covered what is now southern Maryland 17 million years ago. Mounted fossil whales, porpoises, a sea cow, turtles, sharks, and *Pelagornis*, the world's largest fossil bird, are on display.

The most spectacular exhibit in the new hall is the reconstructed jaws of a giant white shark, the larger, fiercer ancestor of today's great white shark. These choppers are even bigger than those of the monster shark in the film *Jaws*. Museum officials hope soon to be able to display a full-scale model of the creature that once owned the fearsome jaws. It would be about 40 feet long. Some 17 million years ago this extinct giant and many of its relatives would have roamed the warm shallow waters of the ancient sea.

This unusually well-run, well-financed regional museum has many nonfossil attractions, from a re-created salt marsh to a lighthouse. But for the fossil hunter the greatest attraction of the region will be the Calvert Cliffs, just a few miles up Route 2 from Solomons. The cliffs, which were once at the bottom of the sea, are loaded with fossils. A visitor can just walk along the shore at the edge of the cliffs and see well-defined layers of fossil shells. The cliffs are eroding rapidly and fossils fall into the surf where they are tossed around, cleaned, and often cast back on the shore. The beaches beneath Calvert Cliffs provide some of the best fossil collecting for the amateur on the East Coast. There are no dinosaur fossils, but bones of ancient whales, porpoises, crocodiles, and other marine creatures have been found. Most of the fossils at Calvert Cliffs are shells. The most popular find is sharks' teeth, which are surprisingly abundant. The reason is that sharks, ancient and modern, have an unlimited supply of teeth and shed them regularly.

Ask at the museum for directions to the public beaches where fossils can be collected and for instructions on how to find and preserve them. You won't need any special tools, just sharp eyes and a bag to carry your finds.

Virginia Living Museum

Where: 524 J. Clyde Morris Boulevard, Newport News, VA 23601

Hours: Memorial Day through Labor Day: Monday through Saturday, 9:00 A.M.-6:00 P.M.; Sunday, 10:00 A.M.-6:00 P.M.; closes one hour earlier during the rest of the year. Open Thursday evenings 7:00 P.M.-9:00 P.M. Closed Thanksgiving, Christmas Eve, Christmas, and New Year's Day.

Admission: Adults $4; Children 3 to 12 years $2. Admission to planetarium is extra.

Phone: (804) 595-1900

This attractive and very active nature center concentrates on the plants and animals of Virginia today. But tucked in between a re-creation of the James River, complete with real fish and other water creatures, and a touch tank where the visitor can handle crabs, starfish, and the like is an exhibit called Virginia's Prehistoric Past. The centerpiece for this exhibit is dinosaur footprints unearthed in 1989 in the Culpeper Stone Quarry near Stevensburg, Virginia. This is not a large exhibit, but the descriptive materials are unusually informative.

Virginia Museum of Natural History

Where: 1001 Douglas Avenue, Martinsville, VA 24122
Hours: Monday through Saturday, 10:00 A.M.-5:00 P.M.; Sunday, 1:00 P.M.-5:00 P.M.
Admission: Adults $2; Children $1.
Phone: (703) 666-8600

This excellent state museum has opened a new Age of Reptiles exhibit. The exhibit contains a computer-controlled model of *Triceratops*, models of some small dinosaurs, and dinosaur tracks. If you are in the museum, be sure to seek out the exhibit on Thomas Jefferson and the natural history of Virginia. Jefferson, America's third president, was also one of the nation's first great fossil collectors.

In the late 1970s workers at the Culpeper Stone Quarry near Stevensburg, Virginia, began to unearth what turned out to be an astonishing array of dinosaur trackways in the siltstone and shale. Some of these tracks are now on display at this museum and others, including the Smithsonian. But isolated tracks are nowhere near as impressive as viewing them in their natural setting. The museum sponsors guided tours to the quarry. This is a unique and thrilling experience for anyone interested in fossils, but no one will be admitted to the quarry without confirmed and prepaid reservations. Information and reservations can be obtained by calling the museum's University of Virginia Branch at (804) 982-2780.

Dinosaur Land

Where: At the intersection of U.S. Routes 522, 340, and 277, between Winchester and Front Royal, VA.

Hours: 9:30 A.M.-5:30 P.M.; open an hour longer in the summer. Closed January 1 to February 28.

Admission: Children up to 10 years $2; everyone over 11 years $2.50

Phone: (703) 869-2222

If you happen to be taking a leisurely drive in the vicinity of Virginia's lovely Shenandoah Valley, and you are a bit of a dinosaur freak, a stop at the roadside attraction called Dinosaur Land could be enjoyable. Don't expect scientific accuracy in these models, which range from a 20-foot *Tyrannosaurus* to a mammoth to King Kong. But you can stretch your legs, grab a snack, take some pretty funny pictures, and experience a piece of real Americana.

WEST VIRGINIA

West Virginia Geological and Economic Survey

Where: Mont Chateau, Mont Chateau Road, Exit 10 (Cheat Lake) off U.S. 48, just north of Morgantown, WV.

Hours: 8:00 A.M.-5:00 P.M. Monday through Friday. Closed on federal and state holidays.

Phone: (301) 594-2331

In 1788 Thomas Jefferson discovered some ancient bones in a cave deposit in what is now Greenbriar County, West Virginia. He published a scientific description of these bones in 1797, when he was vice-president of the United States. The bones were part of the front foot of what Jefferson believed to be a large extinct cat. They turned out to be the remains of a giant ground sloth. In honor of Jefferson's work the animal, *Megalonyx jeffersonii*, was named after him. He is the only U.S. president or vice-president ever to be so honored. Casts of the original Jefferson find are now on display in the lobby of the West Virginia Geological and Economic Survey. Also on display are a variety of other fossils found in the state.

Aurora Fossil Museum

Where: Aurora, NC
Hours: Summer: Tuesday through Friday, 9:00 A.M.-5:00 P.M.; Saturday, 9:00 A.M.-2:00 P.M. Winter: Monday through Friday, 9:00 A.M.-5:00 P.M.
Phone: (919) 322-4238

Most of the fossils in this unique little museum come from the nearby Texasgulf Phosphate Mine. A visit usually begins with a brief slide show about the history of the area and how the fossils were formed and found. Then visitors can look at the cases of fossil shark teeth, whale skulls, and mastodon teeth. A favorite activity is having a picture taken inside a model of gigantic shark jaws. But the most intriguing activity is going on across the street from the museum where there is material from the phosphate mine, which the visitor can sift through in order to find his or her own fossils. Sharks' teeth and fossil shells are common. The museum even provides a guide to the fossils. And it's all free.

North Carolina State Museum of Natural Sciences

Where: 102 N. Salisbury Street, Raleigh, NC 27611
Hours: Monday through Saturday, 9:00 A.M.-5:00 P.M.; Sunday, 1:00 P.M.-4:00 P.M.
Phone: (919) 733-7450

Extensive renovations have been taking place at this museum.

A new fossil lab, where visitors can get a close-up look at how fossils are actually prepared, has been built in the old Fossil Hall. But popular exhibits like a wonderful *Tyrannosaurus* skull, and an equally impressive saber-toothed cat skull will remain on display, no matter what other changes are made. Joining these old favorites will be a replica of the skull and jaw of a *Triceratops*. In the Bird Hall there is an excellent cast of the celebrated *Archaeopteryx* fossil. There are many other delights at this museum. Don't miss the right whale model hanging over the lobby or the full sperm whale skeleton in Marine Mammal Hall. Actually, there is no way you could possibly miss these enormous displays.

North Carolina
Maritime Museum

Where: 315 Front Street, Beaufort, NC 28516, just off Highway 70.

Hours: Monday through Friday, 9:00 A.M.-5:00 P.M.; Saturday, 10:00 A.M.-5:00 P.M.; Sunday, 2:00 P.M.-5:00 P.M.

Phone: (919) 728-5225

Beaufort is a charming and historic seaport town, which has been partially restored for the tourists. Beaufort Harbor is on the Intercoastal Waterway. The Maritime Museum is pri-

marily a ship museum; indeed, the interior gives visitors the feeling of being in the hold of a large wooden ship. But there are some fossils, maritime and otherwise, on display. The museum also has a children's summer program on fossils, and a Fossil Fair in November.

North Carolina Museum
of Life and Science

Where: 433 Murray Avenue, Durham, NC 27704. The museum is ten minutes from downtown Durham just off I-85.

Hours: Monday through Saturday, 10:00 A.M.-5:00 P.M.; Sunday, 1:00 P.M.-5:00 P.M. Open until 6:00 P.M. during the summer. Closed Thanksgiving, Christmas, and New Year's Day.

Admission: Adults $3.75; Children 3 to 12 years $2.75, under 2 years free.

Phone: (919) 477-0431

This is primarily a "hands-on" nature center where visitors can hold a box turtle or look a woodchuck in the eye. For the dinosaur enthusiast there is the Prehistory Trail where a shaded pathway leads past huge models of dinosaurs among the trees and other vegetation. Unfortunately, time and weather have damaged many of these fiberglass models, and museum officials have found that they are virtually impossible to repair. Still, the mastodon and a couple of other models are in pretty good shape, and they are well worth taking a look at. There are also some fossils in the geology exhibit.

South Carolina
State Museum

Where: 301 Gervais Street, Columbia, SC, beside the Gervais Street Bridge and the Congaree River.
Hours: Monday through Saturday, 10:00 A.M.-5:00 P.M. Sunday 1:00 P.M.-5:00 P.M. Closed Christmas Day.
Admission: Adults $3; Seniors, Military, and Students $2; Children 6 to 17 years $1.25, under 6 years free.
Phone: (803) 737-4595

If there is one thing that sticks in the mind of every visitor to this museum it is the model of the prehistoric giant white shark. The 43-foot, 7,000-pound fiberglass-and-aluminum model is suspended from the ceiling of the Natural History Hall. It's an enormous and impressive sight. The hall also contains life-size replicas of the mastodon and *Glyptodon* and a good collection of fossils found within the state. There is an extensive technology exhibit, with everything from the first passenger locomotive built in America to the space suit worn by an astronaut from South Carolina.

The museum is housed in the historic Columbia Mills Building, which opened in 1894 as the first totally electric textile mill. Though the building is old, the museum is new; it opened in 1988 and new exhibits and facilities are still being planned.

The Museum of Arts and Sciences

Where: 4182 Forsyth Road, Macon, GA 31210
Hours: 9:00 A.M.-5:00 P.M. Monday through Thursday and
             Saturday; 9:00 A.M.-9:00 P.M. Friday; 1:00 P.M.-5:00
             P.M. Sunday.
Admission: Adults $2; Students and Seniors $1.
Phone: (912) 477-3232

The pride and joy of this regional museum is Ziggy the *Zygorhiza*, a full reconstruction of the bones of a long-extinct whale. The creature was 18 feet long and possessed a formidable set of jaws and teeth. The vertebrae of a shark, perhaps this carnivorous whale's last meal, were discovered inside its rib cage. The fossil was found in a mine not twenty miles from where it is now on exhibit. Forty million years ago the area near Macon was the shoreline of an ancient ocean. It was discovered in 1973 by a retired railroad man, a local "rock hound" and amateur paleontologist named Bill Christy. The bones were excavated with the help of scientists from the University of Georgia and stored away for years until Christy heard that the Museum of Arts and Sciences was going to expand its building. Money was raised to reconstruct Ziggy and build a permanent exhibit for him (or her). This may be the largest full *Zygorhiza* skeleton on display anywhere in the world. That alone makes The Museum of Arts and Sciences worth a visit.

The museum has displays of everything from folk art to minerals to star shows in an attached planetarium.

Bud Jones Taxidermy

Where: Buchanan Road, Tallapoosa, GA 30176
Phone: (404) 574-7840

A taxidermist usually stuffs the remains of recently dead animals. Bud Jones of Georgia does more. In addition to traditional taxidermy, Bud has been making life-sized models of dinosaurs and other prehistoric creatures for the last few years. His models are generally sold to museums. Bud runs a taxidermy shop, not a tourist attraction, but he's friendly, and if you call ahead and he has the time, he'll probably let you visit and give you a closer, and more personal, look at how these models are made than you are likely to get anywhere else in the country.

FLORIDA

Walt Disney World

Where: Lake Buena Vista, FL
Admission: A great variety of different kinds of tickets and "passports," from single-day tickets to passports good for a full year, are available.
Phone: (407) 824-4321

There are surprisingly few dinosaurs at this enormous entertainment and vacation complex. In the Disney-MGM Studio Theme Park, there is an ice-cream stand in the shape of a dinosaur. The architecture style is California Crazy. The place is called Dinosaur Gertie's Ice Cream of Extinction. It pays homage to Gertie the Dinosaur, star of the first animated cartoon ever made.

Dinosaurs are a more substantial presence at Epcot Center. Exxon's very high-tech Universe of Energy pavilion in the Future World area of Epcot actually gives visitors a very entertaining glimpse into the world of the distant past. The attraction is a clever mixture of entertainment and advertising, like most of the other attractions at Epcot. Visitors start by taking seats in what looks like an ordinary auditorium. Then after a warm-up with computer graphics on giant screens, the auditorium actually divides itself into six 100-passenger "rafts" that drift silently into a primeval swamp where tangled trees and prehistoric ferns form a dense canopy.

The gloom is cut by wind and lightning, startling a dinosaur family munching on swamp grass. A *Brontosaurus* leans out over the visitors as they glide by. Just ahead, a *Stegosaurus* and an *Allosaurus* are locked in combat. The dinosaur's tail lashes out, just missing the raft.

Farther along, a trio of *Ornithomimus* or "bird mimic" dinosaurs struggles to escape from mudholes as the Earth's crust begins turning to desert toward the end of the Age of Dinosaurs. The next scene is a volcanic cataclysm.

The dinosaur models are moved by the audio-animatronic system, familiar to anyone who has ever visited a Disney theme park. The view of dinosaurs as slow-moving swamp dwellers is conventional, perhaps a bit dated, but technically marvelous. One new innovation in this particular exhibit is the "smellitzer machine." The sweet smell of the dinosaur swamp gives way to the acrid smell of molten lava. This adds a new dimension to the experience.

Of course, there is much else to see and experience at Walt Disney World.

Universal Studios Florida

Where: Orlando, FL, near Orlando International Airport. Take
                   I-4 and exit at #29 or #30B, then follow the signs.
Hours: Open every day
Admission: Ticket prices vary from about $30 for a one-day ticket
                   for anyone over 12 to a $90 pass that is good for a full
                   year. There are also special group rates. Parking is extra.
Phone: (407) 363-8000

This is a multimillion-dollar theme park built around the movies. The park's newest and most spectacular ride is based on the *Back to the Future* trilogy. This ride takes the visitor farther back into the past than Doc Brown's original DeLorean ever took Marty McFly. It goes through the Ice Age and farther, to an encounter with a *Tyrannosaurus*. It's all accomplished through exciting state-of-the-art special effects, which are fun, even if you didn't see the original films.

On another ride you can come face to face with the pre-historic though imaginary King Kong, who is still stalking Manhattan. Wandering through the park, visitors may encounter the Flintstones and friends, and in the attraction called "The Fantastic World of Hanna-Barbera" a trip to Flintstones Bedrock City is part of the ride.

There is, of course, much that is not prehistoric at this very classy Disney World competitor.

Museum of Science and History

Where:　　1025 Gulf Life Drive, Jacksonville, FL 32207
Hours:　　 Monday through Thursday, 10:00 A.M.-5:00 P.M.; Friday and Saturday, 10:00 A.M.-6:00 P.M.; Sunday, 1:00 P.M.-6:00 P.M.
Admission: Adults $5; Seniors and Children 4 to 12 years $3; children under 4 years free.
Phone:　　 (904) 396-7062

Formerly the Jacksonville Children's Museum, this institution has a teriffic full *Allosaurus* skeleton in the lobby. There is little else in the way of dinosaur or other fossil material in the museum's permanent exhibit, but changing exhibits are a regular feature here. The museum has already hosted the popular Dinamation robot figures twice.

ALABAMA

Red Mountain Museum

Where: 1421 22nd Street South, Birmingham, AL 35205-4199
Hours: Tuesday through Saturday, 10:00 A.M.-4:30 P.M.; Sunday, 1:00 P.M.-4:30 P.M. Closed Mondays and some holidays.
Admission: $1 donation requested.
Phone: (205) 933-4104 or 933-4124 (24-hour taped message)

For much of Earth's history, what is now Alabama was covered by ancient seas. Visitors can get a graphic look at the layers of rock formed from the ancient sea bottom and the fossils they contain at Birmingham's Landmark Mountain Walk. This is located at what is called the Red Mountain Cut, a place where modern road builders literally cut through the mountain, exposing the area's geological history.

Adjacent to the Landmark Mountain Walk is the small, cheerful, and well-run Red Mountain Museum. The museum contains fossils from all periods of Alabama's history. The pride and joy is the Greene County mosasaur, a fully mounted skeleton of a large marine reptile from the Age of Dinosaurs. This one was found in 1978 in Alabama's Greene County by a museum staff paleontologist.

Other fossils, from shells to a giant sloth skull, are on display, but like so many museums, Red Mountain simply doesn't have the money to adequately exhibit everything it has. For example, in 1982 museum staffers excavated a fairly complete skeleton of an ancient whale. The creature is called *Basilosaurus* because back in the nineteenth century when fossils were first found, it was thought to be a reptile, and the name stuck. Most *Basilosaurus* fossils come from Alabama, and it has been designated the Alabama state fossil. When mounted, Red Mountain Museum's specimen will be 58 feet long. At present the museum is exhibiting only a few of the bones, because it doesn't have the staff or facilities to properly display the whole thing.

There is a dandy model dinosaur in front of Red Mountain Museum, the kind kids like to sit on and have their picture taken. There are picnic grounds, a gift shop, and within walking distance is the Discovery Place, a "hands-on" children's museum.

The DinoStore

Where: 436 Palisades Boulevard, in the Palisades Shopping Center three blocks east of I-65, Birmingham, AL
Hours: 10:00 A.M.-8:00 P.M. Monday through Thursday; 10:00 A.M.-9:00 P.M. Friday and Saturday; noon-6:00 P.M. Sunday
Admission: Store is free. Admission to museum next to the original store: Adults $2; Children $1; Reduced rates for groups.
Phone: (205) 942-DINO (942-3466)

There are scores of places across the country called DinoStore. This is the biggest and, according to owners Deborah and Rick Halbrooks, it is the world's largest single source specialty gift store selling exclusively dinosaur motif merchandise, novelties, authentic collectibles, and just about anything else you can think of that is connected with dinosaurs. The motto is "Gifts of Extinction." Rick has been a dinosaur nut since he was a child, and is a self-proclaimed *"Promo sapiens."*

Next to the original Birmingham store is Rick's Dinosaur Museum, which contains a variety of skeletons and models, and a good deal of Dinosaurabilia, like a re-created Sinclair Oil Company gas station (the *Brontosaurus* was the Sinclair

Oil symbol), dinosaur movie posters, and stamps. There are
some nondinosaur items, like a saber-toothed cat skull. The
couple has either opened, or plans to open, additional stores
in other cities in Alabama and Tennessee. They publish a
quarterly newsletter for customers called *The Pterodactyl
Ptimes*; motto: "Where all the news is old news." The store
sponsors dinosaur slide shows at schools, day care centers, and
anywhere else children gather. One of the store's mascots,
Bertha the Brontosaurus, a 20 foot-long model, is a popular
attraction at parades and other public events. DinoStore is a
place that cries out to be noticed, and it usually is.

What can you get at the DinoStore? You name it, and if it
has to do with dinosaurs this place probably has it. There are
over 200 different dinosaur books, 150 dinosaur figurines, and

120 different dinosaur T-shirts. There are dinosaur rugs, "dinosoap," dinosaur ties and towels, even dinosaur underwear, dinosaur videos and computer programs. There is practically everything you can imagine, and a lot that you never even thought of. For the serious collector there are real fossils, and museum-quality casts. You can even buy a DinoStore, for Rick has begun to offer franchises.

Anniston Museum of Natural History

Where: 4301 McClelland Boulevard, Anniston, AL 36202. Near Interstates 20 and 59, at the intersection of state highway 21 and U.S. 431, two miles north of downtown Anniston.
Hours: Tuesday through Friday, 9:00 A.M.-5:00 P.M.; Saturday, 10:00 A.M.-5:00 P.M.; Sunday, 1:00 P.M.-5:00 P.M. Closed Mondays.
Phone: (205) 237-6766

This is one of the Southeast's finest natural history museums, with an excellent bird collection and an authentic replica of an Alabama cave. The museum also has two real Egyptian mummies. The museum is undergoing extensive reconstruction and expansion, and the dinosaur and dinosaur-related material will be in a new exhibit hall called Dynamic Earth opening in 1992. The old exhibit included an excellent fossil of the fishlike seagoing reptile, ichthyosaur, and a terrific model *Pteranodon* with a 30-foot wingspan. Recent fossil findings indicating that the *Pteranodon* had a furlike skin were duplicated in this model by the use of deer and calf skins. A dinosaur diorama will be central to the new exhibit hall.

LOUISIANA

Audubon Zoo

Where: Between St. Charles Avenue and the Mississippi River in New Orleans, LA. The zoo can be reached from the center of New Orleans by riding the historic St. Charles Avenue streetcar or by a cruise on the Mississippi aboard the stern-wheeler *Cotton Blossom*.

Hours: Weekdays, 9:30 A.M.-4:30 P.M. Open later on weekends April through September.

Admission: Adults $6; Children $3; Infants free

Phone: (504) 861-2537

Dinosaurs at the zoo? There certainly are at this innovative zoo in New Orleans. The exhibit is located in what was once the zoo's aquarium, right between the new reptile house and a still-under-construction bird pavilion. This is a curiously appropriate place, for the small museum called Pathways to the Past stresses the bird-dinosaur link. Centerpiece of this exhibit is a moving, hissing model of a *Coelophysis*, a smallish dinosaur that is considered to be an ancestor of modern birds. The model is familiarly known as Cecil. Another prize in this exhibit is an excellent cast of the fossil of an *Archaeopteryx* that is in the Berlin museum. This is one of the most famous fossils in history, for it clearly shows a creature that is a small dinosaur, yet a dinosaur with wings and feathers. There is a display that compares dinosaur eggs with bird's eggs, and another that explores the pros and cons of the warm-blooded dinosaur theory. This is very much a "hands-on" museum.

LSU Museum of
Geoscience

Where: 109 Howe-Russell Geoscience Complex, Louisiana
             State University, Baton Rouge, LA 70803
Hours: The special dinosaur exhibit is open to the general
             public only on weekends from 10:00 A.M. to 5:00 P.M.
             Weekdays are reserved for schools or other scheduled
             groups.
Admission: Adults $3.50; Seniors $2.50; Children 3 through 17
             years $1.50, under 2 years free.
Phone: (504) 388-GEOS (388-4367). Tour information (504)
             388-2934

For the next several years this campus museum will be home
to a rotating exhibit of the popular Dinamation robotic dinosaurs. There are five models, four of which are changed
every year. In addition to this special exhibit, the museum has
displays of fossils found in the Louisiana area, explanations of
fossil hunting and fossil collecting, and a very unique prehistoric garden. The garden contains plants whose relatives flourished in the Age of Dinosaurs. There is (of course) a DinoStore,
which sells T-shirts, books, models, and other items.

The Museum of Natural Science

Where: In Murphy J. Foster Hall, off Dalrymple Drive on the campus of Louisiana State University, Baton Rouge, LA 70893

Hours: Monday through Friday, 8:00 A.M.-4:00 P.M.; Saturday, 9:30 A.M.-1:00 P.M.

Phone: (504) 388-2855

This is largely a research museum, which means that much of its extensive collection is not on display to the general public. However, there are excellent exhibits of native Louisiana animals, and a modest display of fossil material. Star of the fossil collection is a nearly complete skeleton of an American mastodon found just north of Baton Rouge. There is also an excellent cast of the famous *Archaeopteryx*, which is either a primitive bird or a small feathered dinosaur.

When you finish at The Museum of Natural Science you can stroll the LSU campus and visit some of the university's other museums.

The Dunn-Seiler
Geological Museum

Where: Room 219 Hilburn Hall, on the campus of Mississippi State
             University, State College, MS 39762
Hours: Monday through Friday, 8:00 A.M.-5:00 P.M. Closed major
             holidays.
Phone: (601) 325-3915

The collections in this museum are primarily for teaching and research within the Department of Geology and Geography. Still, there are items which will appeal to the hardcore dinosaur or ancient animal buff. There is a dandy cast of a *Triceratops* skull, and a full cast of the skeleton of a saber-toothed cat. There is also a real fossil of the shell of a giant turtle that once lived in Mississippi. Other exhibits include explanations of how fossils were formed, and what sorts of animals commonly occur as fossils.

The Mississippi Museum
of Natural Science

Where: 111 N. Jefferson Street, Jackson, MS 39202. Take the Pearl
Street Exit off I-55, near the Fairgrounds.
Hours: Monday through Friday, 8:00 A.M.-5:00 P.M.; Saturday,
9:30 A.M.-4:30 P.M.
Phone: (601) 354-7303

The state fossil of Mississippi is *Zygorhiza*, a toothy ancient
whale that lived in the sea that covered Mississippi some 40
million years ago. A particularly fine example of the fossil was
found in Yazoo County in 1971. The 16-foot specimen now
hangs proudly from the ceiling at this museum, which also
features a large aquarium display of current state water creatures. There are a few other fossils, like ancient bison skulls
recovered from the Mississippi River.

Land of Kong
Dinosaur Park

Where: Eight miles west of Eureka Springs, AR. Go west on Highway 62 from Eureka Springs to Highway 187 and follow the "Kong" signs.
Hours: Open daily. Call ahead for hours and rates.
Phone: (501) 253-8113

Billed as "World's Largest Dinosaur Park," this is really a good old-fashioned American roadside attraction. There are about 100 not particularly accurate replicas of prehistoric creatures, real and imagined. Centerpiece is a huge King Kong grasping a life-sized Fay Wray. You can have a picnic, buy souvenirs, park your RV, and go on a hike. Most of all, you can take pictures of the family crawling over those funny-looking dinosaurs. It's not science, but if you are in the vicinity Land of Kong can be fun.

Memphis Pink Palace
Museum

Where: 3050 Central Avenue, Memphis, TN 38111-3399
Hours: Tuesday through Friday, 9:30 A.M.-4:00 P.M.; open
              until 8:30 P.M. on Thursday; Saturday, 9:30 A.M.-5:00
              P.M.; Sunday, 1:00 P.M.-5:00 P.M.
Admission: Adults $3; Children, Students, and Seniors $2; Chil-
              dren under 4 years free
Phone: (901) 320-6320

Everyone wants to know where the name came from. The museum is housed in the pink marble mansion built by grocery magnate Clarence Saunders. A reporter dubbed it the Pink Palace, and the name has stuck, somewhat to the embarrassment of museum officials, who are quick to point out that it is now one of the largest museums in the Southeast.

There are dinosaur tracks, a fine mosasaur fossil, a full mastodon skeleton, and many other fossil remains found in the Memphis area on display in the exhibit called Geology: 4-6 Billion Years of Earth History.

Much of the museum is devoted to the history of the Mid-South. Don't miss a walk-through replica of the world's first self-service grocery store, Clarence Saunders' original Piggly Wiggly store. You won't see that in any other museum.

Frank H. McClung Museum

Where: On the campus of the University of Tennessee, 1327 Circle
Park Drive, Knoxville, TN 37996-3200

Hours: Monday through Friday, 9:00 A.M.-5:00 P.M.; Saturday,
10:00 A.M.-5:00 P.M.; Sunday, 2:00 P.M.-5:00 P.M. Closed
major holidays.

Phone: (615) 974-2144

This is primarily a museum of archaeology, anthropology, and local history. But there are a few fossils of interest, some dinosaur tracks, and Ice Age mammals like a saber-toothed cat skull and a *Glyptodon*, a giant and heavily armored relative of the armadillo.

Cleveland Museum of Natural History

Where: Wade Oval, University Circle, Cleveland, OH 44106
Hours: Monday through Saturday, 10:00 A.M.-5:00 P.M.; Sunday, 1:00 P.M.-5:00 P.M.; Wednesday (September through May), 10:00 A.M.-10:00 P.M. Closed on major holidays.
Admission: Adults $3.75; Children 5 to 17 years, Students, and Seniors $1.75. Under 5 years, no charge. Free admission Tuesday and Thursday, 3:00 P.M.-5:00 P.M.
Phone: (216) 231-4600

One of the scariest-looking creatures that ever existed was not a dinosaur or a saber-toothed cat, it was a fish that lived 360 million years ago. The creature is called *Dunkleosteus terrelli* or "terrible fish." The heavily armored monster could grow to a length of twenty feet, could weigh two tons, and had jaws like meat cleavers. A really fine specimen of this very ancient predator was found in the cliffs of the Rocky River Valley near Cleveland and is on exhibit in the museum.

There are other singular delights to be found in this excellent collection. There is, for example, Happy, the museum's biggest dinosaur and long-time centerpiece of the Kirtland Hall of Prehistoric Life. Happy is a 70-foot-long sauropod, a relative of the *Brontosaurus.* The skeleton was first excavated in Colorado in the 1940s by an expedition from the museum and had been on display for years, but had never been properly identified until quite recently. A reexamination of the material revealed that this was a previously unknown species, and the oldest sauropod found in North America. The creature has been named *Haplocanthosaurus delfsi.*

Another new species "discovered" at the museum is *Nanotyrannus lancensis* ("pygmy tyrant"), which had been improperly identified as a common fossil and relegated to the basement storeroom. The skull of this small relative of the famous *Tyrannosaurus* has been given a place of honor in the dinosaur display. *Nanotyrannus* was one of the most advanced of the meat-eating dinosaurs and some scientists believe it represents a link between dinosaurs and birds.

The museum also contains skeletons of Ice Age mammals like the saber-toothed cat and the American mastodon. In the Hall of Man there is a reproduction of the remains of Lucy, believed to be the oldest and most complete fossil skeleton of a human ancestor.

Cincinnati Museum
of Natural History

Where: Museum Center at Cincinnati Union Terminal. Mail-
              ing address, 1301 Western Avenue, Cincinnati, OH
              45203
Hours: Monday through Saturday, 10:00 A.M.-5:00 P.M.; Sun-
              day, 1:00 P.M.-5:00 P.M. Closed Thanksgiving and
              Christmas.
Admission: Adults $6; Children 3 through 12 years $3.
Phone: (513) 287-7020

In 1990 this museum, which calls itself the oldest scientific
institution west of the Alleghenies, moved to the new Museum
Center in the refurbished Art Deco landmark, Cincinnati's
Union Terminal, the last built of America's great railway sta-
tions. Museum officials have said that the move will catapult
the institution from its status as a medium-sized regional museum to one of the fifteen largest natural history museums in
the United States.

The new facilities opened with a large display of Dinamation's robotic dinosaurs. This display, however, was only temporary. At the end of 1991 the museum opened a major
Pleistocene or Ice Age exhibit, which is one of the showpieces
of the entire Museum Center and one of the best Ice Age
exhibits anywhere. There are one-ton ground sloths, seven-
foot-tall bisons, even a giant beaver, all set up within a realistic
Ice Age landscape that visitors can walk through.

Since the facilities are brand-new, it is vital for visitors to
call ahead for additional information on hours, admission cost,
and simply to find out what's open.

Ohio Historical Center

Where: I-71 and 17th Avenue, Columbus, OH 43211
Hours: Monday through Saturday, 9:00 A.M.-5:00 P.M.; Sunday, 10:00 A.M.-5:00 P.M. Closed Thanksgiving, Christmas, and New Year's Day.
Admission: Free, but there is a $3 parking fee.
Phone: (614) 297-2350

The state of Ohio is rich in mastodon fossils. One of the best found there, or anywhere else, was unearthed in 1894 on the N.S. Conway farm in Clark County, Ohio. This magnificent specimen is on display at the Center. There are a few other fossils, but the mastodon is the star.

KENTUCKY

Big Bone Lick
State Park

Where: On Kentucky Route 338, 25 miles southwest of Cin-
             cinnati, Ohio. Mailing address, 330 Beaver Road,
             Union, KY 41091
Hours: Museum and gift shop open 8:00 A.M.-8:00 P.M. May
             16 to Labor Day. Shorter hours during the rest of the
             year. Closed January.
Admission: The museum charges .50¢ for Adults, .25¢ for Chil-
             dren. Cost of campsites varies.
Phone: (606) 384-3522

During the latter part of the Ice Age many animals—mammoths, mastodons, giant ground sloths, bison, and the like—
would come to the mineral-rich springs of what is now Big
Bone Lick in Kentucky, to drink the water and get the salt and
other minerals they needed. The word "lick" refers to places
where animals go to lick the saline, brackish earth around salt-
mineral springs. An enormous number of these huge creatures
became trapped in the boggy ground around the mineral
springs and perished. The mineral-rich soil helped to preserve
the bones, resulting in one of the richest deposits of Ice Age
mammal remains to be found anywhere in the world.

The bones in this bog were not difficult to find. They were
often right on the surface, and the Indians called the spot "The
Place of Big Bones." In 1739 a French soldier collected some
of these big bones, which were later sent to the French king
for his collection of curiosities. Benjamin Franklin was sent
some bones, which he correctly identified as coming from
elephants (or their close relations). He was puzzled by the fact
that no one had ever seen a living elephant in America.

79

Thomas Jefferson was fascinated by the Big Bone Lick fossils, and he commissioned William Clark of the famous Lewis and Clark expedition to collect bones and have them sent to the White House. This may have been the first organized paleontological expedition in the history of the United States.

The area attracted more than paleontologists. For years salt-making was carried out at Big Bone Lick. During the early 1800s it was a popular resort and spa for Southerners. People believed that drinking the mineral waters was healthy. But the salt-making is long gone, and the spas closed after the Civil War. The marshes are gone and the springs themselves are drying up. Big bones can no longer be found lying about in the mud, but fossils still do turn up, and now this historic area is a state park.

The park has facilities for picnicking, camping, hiking, fishing, and all the usual things one finds in a state park. But there is also a small museum which displays some of the ancient bones and a video-show presentation about the history of Big Bone Lick. Outside there are life-size models of the mastodon and prehistoric bison, the last remaining sulphur spring, and a model "dig" containing bone samples and replicas. Most of all, it gives the visitor a chance to stand at one of the most historically important fossil sites in the United States.

Blue Licks Battlefield State Park

Where: On Kentucky Route 68 between Maysville and Paris. Mailing address, P.O. Box 66, Mount Olivet, KY 41064-0066
Phone: (606) 289-5507

The last battle of the Revolutionary War was fought here; that's why it's a state park. But the area around the mineral springs contained mastodon and other Ice Age bones, much like those found at the more famous and productive Big Bone Lick. A small museum on the grounds features some of the area finds. There are the usual state park amenities.

Behringer-Crawford Museum

Where: In Devou Park, Covington, KY. Mailing address, Box 67, Covington, KY 41012-0067
Hours: Tuesday through Saturday, 10:00 A.M.-5:00 P.M.; Sunday, 1:00 P.M.-5:00 P.M.; Closed Mondays, national holidays, and all of January.
Admission: Adults, $2; Children 4 to 18 years and Seniors $1.
Phone: (606) 491-4003

Devou Park has a golf course, a wonderful overlook of the Ohio River, a summer theater, and a small museum with a fine collection of fossils from Big Bone Lick—better than those actually on display at the site. In addition, the museum will be arranging educational and interpretive programs at Big Bone Lick.

Joseph Moore Museum

Where: On the campus of Earlham College, Richmond, IN 47374
Hours: Monday, Wednesday, and Friday, 1:00 P.M.-4:00 P.M., during the academic year, September to June
Phone: (317) 983-1303

In 1924 there was a disastrous fire which destroyed the building holding the geology and fossil collection of Earlham College. At a critical moment the water supply failed and the fire burned out of control. George Bowles, one of the students, broke into the building and carried out the fossil beaver, no small task since this beaver was as big as a bear. But Bowles knew that this was the only giant beaver skeleton in existence. The mastodon was too large to carry. Fortunately, it was protected from the falling roof by steel beams. Today the giant beaver (still the most complete known skeleton) and the mastodon are on display at the college museum. There is also a small dinosaur and assorted other fossils. Next to the fossils, the Egyptian mummy and a really nice collection of live snakes are the most popular attractions.

The Children's Museum
of Indianapolis

Where: On Meridian Street (U.S. 31) in Indianapolis, IN, bordered by 30th and Illinois streets. Easily accessible from Interstates 65 and 70.

Hours: Between Labor Day and Memorial Day: 10:00 A.M.-5:00 P.M. Tuesday through Saturday; Sunday, noon to 5:00 P.M.; open to 8:00 P.M. Thursdays. Summer hours: 10:00 A.M.-5:00 P.M. Monday through Saturday, noon to 5:00 P.M. Sunday. Closed Thanksgiving, Christmas, and New Year's Day.

Admission: Adults $4; Children 2 to 17 years and Seniors 60 and over $3, under 2 years free. Annual passes and memberships available.

Phone: (317) 924-5431

A life-size *Tyrannosaurus rex* model stands at the front entrance of this beautifully designed and modern gallery to "greet" visitors, and there are over a million of them every year. Inside is a soaring five-story exhibit hall that features the sort of "hands-on" displays that always appeal to children. Permanent exhibits contain everything from an Egyptian mummy to a carousel. There is a mastodon skeleton on display, and a few dinosaur fossils. What is most significant about this museum is that it provides a wonderful place for traveling exhibits, like the robotic dinosaurs. Check what is on temporary display, or just drop by to say hello to *T. rex.*

Field Museum of
Natural History

Where: In Grant Park on Chicago's lakefront, easily reached by car or public transportation.
Hours: Daily 9:00 A.M.-5:00 P.M. Closed Thanksgiving, Christmas, and New Year's Day.
Admission: Adults $3; Children 2 to 17 years, Seniors, and Students with I.D.s $2. Free on Thursdays.
Phone: (312) 922-9410

One of America's great natural history museums, many of the exhibits at the Field Museum are currently undergoing major modernizations and renovations. Renovations of the gallery of dinosaurs and fossil mammals are scheduled for completion sometime in 1993, the museum's one-hundredth anniversary.

If you are going to the Field Museum specifically to see the dinosaur exhibit, it's best to call ahead and find out what is actually open in order to avoid disappointment.

One thing that will be on display no matter when you go is the huge *Albertosaurus* skeleton in the main hall. The creature towers over its prey, the remains of a *Lambeosaurus*. Both dinosaurs lived in Canada some 75 million years ago.

Dominating the old dinosaur display, and almost certainly destined to dominate the new one as well, is the 80-foot-long skeleton of *Apatosaurus*, better known as *Brontosaurus*. Be sure to read the information detailing the checkered history of this particular specimen.

The museum's collection of prehistoric mammal skeletons and models (mastodon, mammoth, saber-toothed cat, giant ground sloth, and the like) is even better than its dinosaur collection, and should not be overlooked in the rush to see the dinosaurs.

Not to be missed are the prehistoric life murals by Charles R. Knight, the greatest paleontological artist ever. Though many features of the Knight paintings are now considered dated, in view of the many discoveries and new theories of the past fifty years, his vision of life in the Age of Dinosaurs and the prehistoric mammals dominated the view of generations, and for good reason. Dated or not, these pictures are simply terrific. Museum officials promise that during renovations the Knight murals will be cleaned and moved from the poorly lit back walls where they are now shown to eye level where they can be more fully appreciated.

The Field Museum has an excellent shop and bookstore, not to mention world-class exhibits of everything from gems to Egyptology.

The Museum of the Chicago Academy of Sciences

Where: 2001 North Clark Street, Chicago, IL 60614
Hours: Open daily 10:00 A.M.-5:00 P.M. Call for summer hours. Closed Christmas Day.
Admission: Adults $1; Children 6 to 17 years, and Seniors .50¢. Free for children under 6 years and free on Monday for everybody. There may be a charge for special exhibits.
Phone: (312) 871-2668

Primarily a museum with displays of the natural history of the Chicago region, the Academy has some dinosaur puzzles and other activities in its Children's Gallery, and a Dinosaur Alcove with more games and puzzles. More significantly, this institution has sponsored a number of traveling dinosaur exhibits. Robotic dinosaurs have made several appearances, and it was one of the early stops for Dinamation's "Prehistoric Sea Monsters" exhibit. There are also lectures and other activities, some of which concern dinosaurs.

The Fryxell Geology Museum

Where: Located in the New Science Building on the campus of Augustana College, Rock Island, IL 61201

Hours: Monday through Friday, 8:00 A.M.-5:00 P.M.; Saturday and Sunday, 1:00 P.M.-4:00 P.M. Closed major holidays.

Phone: (309) 794-8513

A small, friendly, and thoroughly charming museum that welcomes visitors, but prefers they call in advance, particularly if they want a guided tour. The museum's oldest fossil is the remains of 2 billion-year-old single-celled algae. The youngest is a passenger pigeon, a bird that became extinct in 1914. How can a stuffed bird be a fossil? The museum's guide quite correctly points out that a fossil is any evidence of former life. Between these two extremes are full or partial remains of trilobites, mammoths, a 16 foot-long mososaur, an extinct kangaroo, and several species of dinosaurs. The museum is particularly proud of its recent acquisition of a fine *Triceratops* skull from eastern Montana. There is also a *Tyrannosaurus rex* skull and the curious skull of a "bone-headed" dinosaur. A museum of this size cannot have a collection that even comes close to those displayed in the major museums, but here, as in many of the better small museums, the visitor can get up close to the exhibits and take the time to really look at them, and have someone answer questions about them. This part of the museum experience is often lost in the larger institutions, but it is alive and well at the Fryxell Geology Museum. When the visit to the museum is finished you can go to the John Deere Planetarium right next door.

Aurora Historical Museum

Where: 317 Cedar Street, Aurora, IL 60506
Hours: Wednesday through Sunday, 1:00 P.M.-5:00 P.M.
Phone: (708) 897-9029

In 1934, in the depths of the Great Depression, the U.S. government established the Public Works Administration to give jobs to people who were out of work, and to build parks and other public facilities that were needed. One of the projects was to build a lake in Phillips Park in Aurora, Illinois. In January, 1934, the work crew found some big bones, "too large to be from a horse or cow." The bones turned out to be the remains of several mastodons. The Field Museum in Chicago wanted to get the bones for exhibit, but the people of Aurora were proud of what they had found, and wanted the bones to stay where they had been found. So they were given a permanent home in the Aurora Historical Museum. The museum was founded to display objects that trace the history of the town. There is, for example, a fine display of Victorian furnishings, clothing, and decorative arts. But the most popular exhibit is those bones.

MICHIGAN

Exhibit Museum

Where: On the campus of the University of Michigan. Ruthven Museum Building, 1109 Geddes Avenue, Ann Arbor, MI 48109-1079

Hours: Tuesday through Saturday, 9:00 A.M.-5:00 P.M.; Sunday, 1:00 P.M.-5:00 P.M. Closed Mondays and major holidays.

Admission: Free, but donations are appreciated and encouraged.

Phone: (313) 764-0478

The entire second floor of this excellent university museum is called the Hall of Evolution, and is devoted entirely to prehistoric life, from early invertebrates to human evolution. Dinosaurs abound here with full skeletons of many of the most famous and popular dinosaurs on display. In one dramatic display *Allosaurus* stands over the skeleton of *Stegosaurus*. Just behind this exhibit the remains of *Anatosaurus*, a large duck-billed dinosaur, lie on their side just as they were found. Bones of *Tyrannosaurus rex* and *Brontosaurus* (or *Apatosaurus*) can also be seen. The fossil mammals in the collection are generally those found in Michigan, like the mastodon and the five-foot-tall giant beaver.

Cranbrook Institute
of Science

Where: 500 Lone Pine Road, Box 801, Bloomfield Hills, MI 48013

Hours: Monday through Friday, 10:00 A.M.-5:00 P.M., also open from 7:00 P.M.-10:00 P.M. Friday evenings; Saturday, 10:00 A.M.-10:00 P.M.; Sunday, 1:00 P.M.-5:00 P.M. Closed major holidays.

Admission: Adults $3; Children 3 to 17 years and Seniors $2.

Phone: (313) 645-3200

No visit to this institution is complete without a picture of the kids next to the full-size fiberglass model of a *Stegosaurus* that stands outside. Inside there is a display of dinosaur tracks, some mastodon remains, and a cast of Lucy, generally regarded to be the oldest known direct human ancestor.

WISCONSIN

Milwaukee Public Museum

Where:　　800 West Wells Street, Milwaukee, WI 53233
Hours:　　Monday, noon-3:00 P.M.; Tuesday through Sunday,
　　　　　　9:00 A.M.-5:00 P.M.
Admission:　Adults $4; Children 4 to 17 years and Seniors $2; Family rate, $10.
Phone:　　(414) 278-2702

In 1981 paleontologists and volunteers from this museum were on a Dig-a-Dinosaur expedition to northeastern Montana. They were looking for new fossils to display in Geology Hall. Their success was spectacular, for they found the remains of a *Torosaurus* ("bull lizard"). It is a close relative of the more familiar *Triceratops*. *Torosaurus* specimens are rare, but what makes this one truly unique is that it has the world's largest dinosaur skull, more than 9 feet long from the tip of the beak to the back of the frill, and 8 feet wide. The expedition also found the first known skeletal bones of the creature, including front limbs, ribs, and vertebrae. The *Torosaurus* reconstruction has taken place in public, right in the museum lobby where visitors could touch a dinosaur bone and question staff members about what they were doing.

There are other dinosaur fossils on display, including a pair of rare and unusual skulls of the bone-headed dinosaur *Pachycephalosaurus*. The two skulls are the only known ones of their kind in the world. There is also a very popular diorama reconstruction of *Tyrannosaurus* attacking *Triceratops*.

The collection of Ice Age mammal specimens features the first examples of mastodon hair ever found. The specimens were discovered near Milwaukee's Mitchell International Airport. Before the discovery it was believed that mastodons had long, coarse, stringy hair. In reality, their hair was fine, short, and dense.

Geology Museum, University of Wisconsin-Madison

Where: On the University of Wisconsin-Madison campus, 1215 West Dayton Street, Madison, WI 53706
Hours: Monday through Friday, 8:30 A.M.-4:30 P.M.; Saturday, 9:00 A.M.-1:00 P.M.
Phone: (608) 262-1412

Until recently this small museum tucked away in a university building was known primarily for its exhibit of Ice Age mammals. The symbol of the museum was the Boaz mastodon, an excellent fossil found in 1897 near Boaz in Richland County, Wisconsin. A stone spear point was reportedly found with the skeleton, suggesting that the animal had been killed by early Indian hunters. This, according to the museum, was the first reasonably reliable record of an American mastodon found together with a human artifact. The museum also had (and still has) a first-rate titanothere exhibit. Titanotheres were elephant-sized relatives of the rhinoceros. Another popular exhibit is the *Glyptodon*, a relative of the armadillo about the size of a Volkswagen Beetle.

During the 1980s, expeditions by university students and volunteers in various parts of the country turned up some impressive fossils, two of which have been restored and mounted. The first to go up was an 18-foot-long marine reptile, a mosasaur, now suspended from the museum ceiling. At the end of 1990 the museum unveiled its newest prize, a full reconstruction of a 35-foot-long skeleton of a duck-billed dinosaur *Edmontosaurus*.

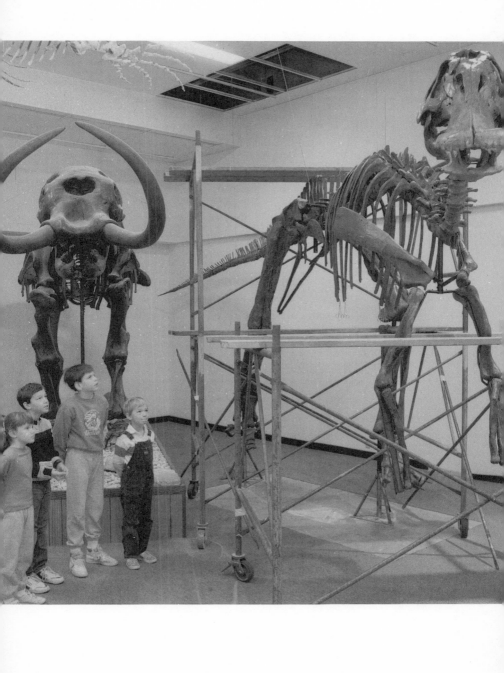

The Science Museum
of Minnesota

Where: 30 East Tenth Street, Saint Paul, MN 55101
Hours: Monday through Saturday 9:30 A.M.-9:00 P.M.; Sunday, 11:00 A.M.-9:00 P.M.
Admission: Adults $3.50; Children 12 years and under and Seniors $2.50. Special exhibits or shows may cost extra.
Phone: (612) 221-9488 Twenty-four-hour recorded message (612) 221-9454

A couple of rarely seen ancient crocodiles are the fossils that this museum is most proud of. But there are plenty of dinosaurs, a half dozen full skeletons or life-size restorations, and lots of other goodies like dinosaur eggs, and a cast of a *Tyrannosaurus rex* skull. In addition, there is a nice selection of fossil mammal skeletons. At the present time the museum's popular Hall of Paleontology is being completely refurbished. All of the old exhibits are being moved, and new ones will be added. The project is scheduled to be completed sometime in 1994. In the meantime, the museum has what they call the Visible Lab where visitors can actually watch the preparation and mounting of the fossils.

University of Iowa
Museum of Natural History

Where: On the campus of the University of Iowa, Iowa City, IA
52242
Hours: Monday through Saturday, 9:30 A.M.-4:30 P.M. Closed on
University and national holidays.
Phone: (319) 335-0480

In the museum's Iowa Hall Gallery there is an Ice Age mammal exhibit. The exhibit is divided into three sections labeled
"Extinct," "Extant," and "Emigrant." Line drawings are in
the background and actual skulls, tusks, and antlers are in the
foreground, indicating the animals which lived in Iowa during
that time period. There is also a nine-foot-tall reconstruction
of a giant ground sloth, which browsed Iowa's woodlands during the Ice Age.

Mastodon State Park

Where: 1551 Seckman Road, Imperial, MO 63052
Hours: Visitor Center open 9:00 A.M.-4:30 P.M. Monday through Saturday; Sunday, noon-4:30 P.M. Park closes one half hour after sunset.
Phone: (314) 464-2976

This area, once known as Sulpher Springs or the Kimmswick Bone Beds, was first investigated by the colorful Dr. Albert C. Koch in 1839. Koch, part scientist, part fraud, and all show-man, found the remains of a number of fossil mammals, primarily mastodons. He claimed that he discovered an en-tirely new creature, a strange-looking aquatic animal he called *Missourium kochii* or the Missouri leviathan. He took the bones of his monster on tour, and finally sold them, for a huge sum, to the British Museum. There they were correctly reassembled as one of the best American mastodon skeletons ever found.

After Koch, a lot of people, qualified and unqualified, began digging in these rich fossil beds, and many of the finds were sold, given away, taken by relic hunters, or destroyed in a later limestone quarrying operation. By 1970 people in the area began to fear that this important site might vanish completely. So, led by four local women, a campaign was begun to raise funds to purchase the site and turn it into a state park. By 1976 Mastodon State Park had been created.

The most important discovery made at the site came in 1979 when excavators found a large stone spear point in direct as-sociation with mastodon bones. According to park officials, this was the first time that scientists had solid evidence of the coexistence of men and mastodons in eastern North America.

Work still goes on from time to time today, and visitors may sometimes be able to view an excavation in progress.

There is a Visitor Center at the park which has a life-size replica of a mastodon skeleton, exhibits showing what the area was like 12,000 years ago when the fossils beds were formed, and the history of excavations. There is a short trail that leads to the site where the bones and human artifacts were discovered.

A shady picnic area near a small creek, and a number of attractive and not too taxing hiking trails are found within the boundaries of the park.

St. Louis Science Center

Where: 5050 Oakland Avenue, St. Louis, MO 63110
Phone: (314) 289-4400 or (314) 289-4444. Recorded message gives
           hours and admission prices.

Outside of the Center is a small picnic area called Dinosaur Park, which gets its name from its most prominent residents, large models of *Tyrannosaurus rex* and *Triceratops*. A new exhibit, opened in late 1991, features larger models of the same two dinosaur species, plus a *Pteranodon* gliding overhead. A dinosaur video show uses old film clips to dispel myths about dinosaurs and provide information on some twenty dinosaur species. In addition, there are exhibits depicting the St. Louis region before and after the Age of Dinosaurs, including the period when Missouri was at the bottom of the sea, and the land and its inhabitants during the Ice Age.

KANSAS

Museum of Natural History

Where: In Dyche Hall on Jayhawk Boulevard, on the University
of Kansas campus, Lawrence, KS 66045-2454
Hours: Monday through Saturday, 8:00 A.M.-5:00 P.M.; Sundays
and holidays, 1:00 P.M.-5:00 P.M. Closed New Year's Day,
4th of July, Thanksgiving, and Christmas.
Phone: (913) 864-4540 weekdays, (913) 864-4450 weekends

During much of the time in which dinosaurs roamed the earth,
Kansas was covered by a shallow sea. For that reason, dinosaur
fossils are rare, but fossils of large marine reptiles and pterosaurs
are abundant and world-famous. Some of the best of the Kansas
fossils are housed in this museum, making it one of the nation's
leading paleontological museums. On the third floor the visitor
will find the most extensive collection of ichthyosaurs, mosasaurs, plesiosaurs, phytosaurs, and giant turtles he or she is
likely to encounter anywhere.

Though partial remains of the largest-known flying reptile,
one of the pterosaurs, have been found in Texas, the largest
full skeleton of a pterosaur was found in Kansas and is on
display in this museum. It is *Pteranodon* with its 25-foot wing-
spread. The jaws of this exotic-looking creature consisted of a
long, toothless beak; the back of the skull extended backwards
as a crest, which scientists believe balanced the weight of the
large beak. Some flying reptile fossils have imprints of hair on
their skin, causing scientists to speculate that they were "warm-
blooded," a speculation that has also been made about the
dinosaurs.

The pterosaurs were not birds and are not ancestors to birds,
but there are some real birds from the Age of Dinosaurs in

this collection as well. There are, for example, models of *Hesperornis*, an ancient toothed bird adapted for swimming and diving, and *Ichthyornis*, a ternlike bird that also had teeth. These creatures often are not shown, even in good museum collections, but they are well represented in this one.

There are a few dinosaurs, the armored dinosaurs (ankylosaurs) and duck-billed dinosaurs (hadrosaurs) that have been found in Kansas, and some from other regions as well.

Notable among the fossil mammals on exhibit is a mounted skeleton of *Teleoceras*, a hornless rhinoceros. There are mammoths and mastodons and other Pleistocene or Ice Age fossils from Kansas, and an excellent exhibit of fossils from the famous La Brea Tar Pits in California. An historic skeleton on display is that of an extinct bison, much larger than the modern bison. What makes this particular specimen historic, museum officials say, is that it is the first extinct animal ever to be found in association with an Indian artifact in North America. Scientists found a spear point between the creature's ribs. Unfortunately, the spear point was later stolen.

This is not a flashy museum, but it has an extensive and unique collection, and it should not be missed if you find yourself anywhere in the vicinity.

The Sternberg Memorial Museum

Where: On the first floor of McCartney Hall, on the campus of Fort Hays State University, Hays, KS 67601-4099
Hours: Weekdays, 9:00 A.M.-5:00 P.M.; Saturdays and Sundays, 1:00 P.M.-5:00 P.M. Closed major holidays.
Phone: Toll-free number in Kansas 1-800-432-0248, ext. 4286. Out of state (913) 628-4286.

Some 90 million years ago, when an inland sea covered what is now Kansas, a large sea fish called *Xiphactinus* swallowed a somewhat smaller fish, *Gillicus*. The larger fish then promptly died, before its prey was digested. Perhaps it choked on its last big meal. It sank to the bottom of the sea and was quickly buried by mud, preserving both specimens in nearly perfect position. There they both remained until uncovered by scientists in 1952. The fossilized remains of prey have been found inside of carnivorous fish and other predators, but in no other specimen have predator and prey been preserved so perfectly. This fossil of a "fish within a fish" became world-famous. The original is on display in the museum at Fort Hays State University, not far from where it was found.

While the "fish within a fish" is far and away the most celebrated fossil in this museum, there are many other fossils worth seeing. Because Kansas was covered with water during the Age of Dinosaurs there are few dinosaur fossils here, but there are excellent examples of large marine and flying reptiles from that period. From Ice Age Kansas there are mammoth and mastodon remains, as well as fossil camels, horses, rhinoceros, bison, musk-oxen, and the giant ground sloth.

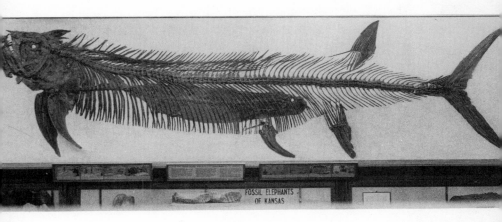

NEBRASKA

Morrill Hall

Where: On the campus of the University of Nebraska, 14th and U streets, Lincoln, NE 68588

Hours: Monday through Saturday, 9:30 A.M.-4:30 P.M.; Sunday and holidays, 1:30 P.M.-4:30 P.M. Closed Christmas and New Year's Day.

Admission: Voluntary, but $1 for Adults and .50¢ for Children and Students is suggested.

Phone: (402) 472-2642

Elephant Hall is one of the names by which this museum is known, and for good reason. It has one of the best collections of fossil elephants anywhere in the world. There is the Prod tusker, Shovel tusker, Scoop tusker, Perfect tusker, Short-jawed tusker, American mastodon, Dwarf mammoth, Imperial mammoth, and Jefferson's mammoth, all on display here. Star of the collection is the skeleton of *Archidiskodon* (Archie for short), the largest mounted elephant in existence. This giant, over 14 feet tall, roamed Nebraska some 70,000 years ago.

Extinct elephants aren't the only fossils to be seen. Nebraska is exceptionally rich in fossil mammals of all sorts. There are exhibits on the evolution of the rhinoceros and the horse. There are examples of the giant camel, the giant beaver, a variety of ground sloths, a reconstruction of *Baluchitherium*, the world's largest terrestrial mammal, and much, much more.

In the realm of superlatives the museum has on display the longest-necked plesiosaur in the world. There is another sea-going reptile, a 20-foot-long mosasaur; no record, but still impressive. There is also an excellent specimen of a long-tailed pterosaur. But what about dinosaurs? Since Nebraska, like much of that region of the United States, was underwater during the Age of Dinosaurs, fossils of these land-living creatures are rare. However, there are some striking imports, including full, mounted skeletons of both *Allosaurus* and *Stegosaurus*.

Only a tiny percentage of the museum's specimens are on display. Most are housed in what is called the museum's Systematic Collections and are not open to the public. Members of the Friends of the Museum are given an annual tour of this amazing facility.

There are some renovations going on at the museum, and plans call for more in the future, so it might be wise to telephone ahead and check if you are thinking about a visit.

Agate Fossil Beds
National Monument

Where: Twenty-three miles south of U.S. 20 at Harrison, NE via
Nebraska 29, or 34 miles north of U.S. 26 at Mitchell, via
Nebraska 29. Mailing address, HC 79, Box 9, Harrison,
NE 69346

Phone: (308) 668-2211

In 1885 James Cook found what he described as "a beautifully
petrified piece of the shaft of some creature's leg bone" on his
ranch in western Nebraska. It was several years before the find
was shown to scientists. Once the scientists visited Cook's
ranch, they realized that it contained one of the richest fossil
sites in America. This was the period in which fossil discoveries
in the American West provoked a virtual frenzy of excavation.
Many of the world's leading paleontologists, including those
two notorious rivals Edward Drinker Cope of Philadelphia and
Othniel Charles Marsh of Yale University were guests at Cook's
Agate Springs Ranch, though on separate occasions. A more
gentlemanly rivalry took place between scientists from the University of Nebraska and the Carnegie Museum in Pittsburgh.
Two of the main fossil areas are called University Hill and
Carnegie Hill.

The Cook family actively encouraged scientific exploration
and would often take tourists to visit the fossil sites on summer
weekends. In 1965 the family got the United States government
to add the fossil beds to the National Park System.

The Agate Fossil Beds do not contain the remains of dinosaurs. They were formed some 19 million years ago, during
what is frequently referred to as the Age of Mammals. The
number of species found at this site is truly remarkable. The
most common mammal found at Agate Fossil Beds was *Me-
noceras*, a two-horned rhinoceros a bit smaller than a pony.
The strangest-looking was *Moropus*, a large heavily built an-

imal with a horselike head and neck, the front legs of a rhinoceros, the hind legs of a bear, and enormous claws. The combination is so unusual that scientists first believed that the bones of several different species had been mixed together. Possibly the most ferocious creature to be found was *Dinohyus* or "terrible pig." It was more than seven feet high at the shoulders and ten feet long, with a massive head and large tusks. It was probably an aggressive creature, for fossils indicate that a large number of them were wounded.

There is a Visitor Center that has exhibits on the fossils and the history of scientific exploration at the fossil beds. Nearby is a self-guided trail to an area of exposed fossils. The National Park Service is planning to build more permanent structures and make the site more accessible to tourists. If you want to see the place very much as it looked to Cope and Marsh, you'd better hurry. It has been estimated that 75 percent of the fossils in the Agate Beds remain unexcavated, and expeditions from various universities and museums can often be found at work.

There are no facilities at the monument for camping. Restaurants and overnight accommodations are available in nearby towns. Visitors are warned that everything from fossils to plants is protected, and no collecting is allowed. Visitors are also warned that there are plenty of rattlesnakes in the fossil areas, so watch out.

Trailside Museum

Where: At Fort Robinson State Park, two miles west of Crawford, NE, on Highway 20
Hours: Open Memorial Day through Labor Day. Monday through Saturday, 8:00 A.M.-5:00 P.M.; Sunday 9:00 A.M.-5:00 P.M.
Phone: (308) 665-2730

Run by the University of Nebraska, this small facility has a fine Columbian mammoth skeleton and other Ice Age fossils. Most importantly, it is a center for well-conducted and modestly priced daily trips to some of the impressive fossil sites of western Nebraska and South Dakota.

Southwest

TEXAS

Dinosaur Valley State Park

Where: About four miles north of Glen Rose, TX
Hours: Open every day, weather permitting.
Admission: $2 per car for day visitors. Additional fee for campsites.
Phone: (817) 897-4588

Probably the most famous dinosaur tracks in the world are those to be seen in this park, on the banks of the Paluxy River. Natural erosion of the bed and banks has laid bare many footprints on the surfaces of several hard layers of limestone. This area was once part of the seacoast, and dinosaurs left their footprints in the limey mud of the coast. Three types of dinosaurs appear to have left their prints. There were the gigantic sauropods, like *Brontosaurus*, large two-legged carnivores, and lightly built two-legged plant eaters.

The Indians and early white setters were quite familiar with the prints. Blocks of limestone with good prints were chiseled out and sold to curiosity seekers, and occasionally to museums. A set of spectacular tracks from this area is on display in the American Museum of Natural History in New York City. Local craftsmen also made and sold phony tracks. Today the tracks are completely protected as part of a state park and the site was designated a National Natural Landmark by the National Park Service in 1969.

The tracks gained some notoriety when it was rumored that human tracks had been found scattered among the dinosaur footprints. Creationists who believe that the world is only a few thousand years old pointed to the "human footprints" as proof that men and dinosaurs had lived at the same time. However, scientists are convinced that the so-called "human footprints" are really those of a lightweight two-legged dinosaur. Some Creationist leaders have backed away from the idea of "human footprints." But accounts of the "human footprints" along the Paluxy River still turn up regularly in Creationist literature, and have helped to spread the fame of this particular site.

Dinosaur Valley State Park provides excellent facilities for visitors who want to view the clearly marked tracks in the bed and banks of the river. They are very visible except during periods when the river is swollen.

In 1970 an oil company donated the life-sized fiberglass models of *Brontosaurus* and *Tyrannosaurus*, created by the artist Louis Paul Jonas and previously on display at the New York World's Fair, to the Park, where they can still be seen.

Houston Museum of Natural Science

Where: One Hermann Circle Drive across from the Miller
              Outdoor Theatre, Houston, TX 77030
Hours: Monday through Saturday, 9:00 A.M.-6:00 P.M.; Sun-
              day, noon-6:00 P.M.
Admission: Adults $2.50; Children $2.
Phone: (713) 639-4600

A 70-foot-long, two-story-tall skeleton of *Diplodocus*, the longest-known dinosaur, dominates the main hall of this museum. There is also an excellent new fossil mammal display which shows *Dinictis felina*, an early saber-toothed cat, as it leaps on *Mesohippus*, a small ancestor of the modern horse. Unlike other saber-toothed cats, which were heavy, *Dinictis* was probably light and fast enough to catch speedy prey such as the horse in this exhibit. In addition to the permanent exhibits, the museum has often been home to traveling exhibits like the robotic dinosaurs and the "Treasures of the Tar Pits."

Dallas Museum of Natural History

Where: Fair Park, Second and Grand avenues, off Route I-30. This institution is also called The Science Place. Mailing address, P.O. Box 26193, Dallas, TX 75226

Hours: Daily 9:00 A.M.-5:00 P.M. Closed Thanksgiving and Christmas Day.

Admission: Suggested donation $1. There may be an extra fee for special exhibits.

Phone: (214) 670-8457

The most impressive single specimen in this regional museum's Prehistoric Texas hall is a 31-foot mosasaur, an aquatic reptile from the Age of Dinosaurs. This one, called the Heath mosasaur for the Texas town near which it was found in 1979, is considered one of the finest fossils of its type. It was discovered quite by accident by a family sailing on a local lake. They took a piece of the bone to the museum where it was identified, and the fossil was then excavated by members of the museum staff and volunteers.

Also on display are fossils of *Tenontosaurus*, a recently identified dinosaur that appears to have been fairly common in Texas 115 million years ago. A nice specimen was found in Wise County, about a two-hour drive from Dallas.

There is a good selection of Ice Age mammal fossils, including the 13-foot-tall Trinity mammoth, so named because it was discovered in a sand and gravel pit at the Trinity River in Dallas.

Fort Worth Museum of Science and History

Where: 1501 Montgomery Street, Fort Worth, TX 76107
Hours: Monday, 9:00 A.M.-5:00 P.M.; Tuesday through Thursday, 9:00 A.M.-8:00 P.M.; Friday and Saturday, 9:00 A.M.-9:00 P.M.; Sunday, noon-8:00 P.M. Closed Labor Day, Thanksgiving, Christmas Eve, Christmas Day, New Year's Day, and 4th of July.
Admission: Adults, $3; Children 5 to 12 years and Seniors $1; Children under 5 years free. A pass can be purchased that is good for an entire month.
Phone: (817) 732-1631

In 1988 the full and partial skeletons of at least three individual *Tenontosaurus* dinosaurs were found by a local biology teacher and his son on a ranch near Fort Worth. The *Tenontosaurus* was a seven-foot-tall, twenty-foot-long plant eater. This find was so well preserved that it will add a great deal to scientific understanding of this particular creature. Scientists from the Fort Worth Museum helped excavate the discovery, and the *Tenontosaurus* is the most important specimen in the museum's modest dinosaur exhibit. The museum is now planning to expand its paleontological display.

Brazosport Museum of Natural Science

Where: 400 College Drive, Lake Jackson, TX 77566
Hours: Tuesday through Saturday, 10:00 A.M.-5:00 P.M.; Sunday, 2:00 P.M.-5:00 P.M. Closed Monday.
Phone: (409) 265-7831

The pride of this enthusiastically supported local museum is the largest collection of shells in the southern United States. Next is its 25-foot-long model of an *Allosaurus* skeleton. There are other fossils from the Texas Gulf and coastal regions. The museum provides lectures, demonstrations, and tours, as well as an identification service for fossils, shells, and other natural objects.

Robert A. Vines Environmental Science Center

Where: 8856 Westview Drive, Houston, TX 77055
Hours: Monday through Friday, 8:30 A.M.-5:00 P.M.
Phone: (713) 465-9628

In this very pleasant setting the visitor can stroll through the five-acre arboretum and bird sanctuary, the home of some 200 native species of trees, shrubs, and vines, then go into the geology hall and come face to face with a 33-foot-long *Allosaurus* skeleton. There are also such things as *Brontosaurus* footprints, a *Tyrannosaurus* skull, and a good explanation of how the process of fossilization occurs.

Museum of Texas
Tech University

Where: Fourth and Indiana Avenue, Lubbock, TX 79409
Hours: Tuesday through Saturday, 10:00 A.M.-5:00 P.M. Open until 8:30 P.M. on Thursday. Sunday, 1:00 P.M.-5:00 P.M. Closed Monday.
Phone: (806) 742-2490

Devoted to preserving the cultural heritage of the Southwest, this may be the only museum in the world with a large Ranching Heritage Center. But there were animals in the Southwest before the cattle arrived and some of them were dinosaurs. There is an *Allosaurus* on display in the main museum building, along with some other dinosaur fossils, and an excellent Columbian mammoth skull. There is also a huge mural showing life in West Texas from prehistoric to modern times. Dinosaurs dominate the scene. The museum has a lot of good fossil material that is not on display. In 1980 an expedition from the university discovered a rich fossil site near Post, Garza County, in West Texas. The site has yielded the remains of at least a dozen individual dinosaurs, including a previously unknown dinosaur named *Postosuchus*. This creature is believed to be the ancestor of the famous *Tyrannosaurus rex*. A much more elaborate gallery for these important finds is in the planning stage.

Big Bend National Park

Where: The Rio Grande forms the southern border of this remote park in southwestern Texas. It is not near any
major urban centers. The closest towns in Texas are
Marathon, Alpine, and Study Butte. Mailing address,
Big Bend National Park, TX 79834

Hours: The park is open year-round, but can be particularly
crowded during Easter/Spring break, Thanksgiving,
and Christmas. Then the main campgrounds are likely
to be full.

Admission: $5 per vehicle allows entry for one week. There are a
variety of long-term admission fees, plus a variety of
extra fees for camping.

Phone: Headquarters (915) 477-2251

Late in 1971 a University of Texas graduate student conducting
a field investigation at the park for his master's thesis happened
to spot an unusual-looking fragment of fossil bone. The bone
turned out to be part of the wing of the largest flying creature
ever discovered, a gigantic pterosaur which has been named
Quetzalcoatlus for the Aztec god that appeared in the form of
a feathered serpent. This Texas pterosaur would have had a
wingspan of some 50 feet, twice as big as the biggest pterosaur
then known and far larger than any other known flying creature. Prior to the discovery, scientists did not believe that
anything that large could fly. Even today there are many un-
answered questions about how this giant was able to get up in
the air, and land.

No paleontological discovery in years has attracted so much
popular attention and wonder. Since the original discovery,
partial fossils of some smaller specimens of the same species
have been found nearby.

There are no monuments to this flying monster at the spot
where it was discovered, but on the floor of the Visitor Center

there is the shadow of the 50-foot wingspan. The park is also beginning to include more about paleontology in its regular naturalist programs.

A reminder to potential tourists, Big Bend is a remote and rugged area, so a trip here takes some planning.

Texas Memorial Museum

Where: On the campus of the University of Texas at Austin, 2400 Trinity Street, Austin, TX 78705
Hours: Monday through Friday, 9:00 A.M.-5:00 P.M.; Saturday, 10:00 A.M.-5:00 P.M.; Sunday, 1:00 P.M.-5:00 P.M.
Phone: (512) 471-1604

Since the celebrated giant pterosaur fossil was found by a University of Texas graduate student, it is only fitting that the centerpiece of the paleontology exhibit is a cast of the original fossil. Overall, the museum has an excellent pterosaur exhibit.

In a small building just outside the main museum are dinosaur tracks from Paluxy Creek, Texas. Hanging near the main entrance is a 30-foot mosasaur, found near Austin. Inside the crowded Paleontology Hall are a *Diplodocus* thighbone, fossils of giant and very ancient amphibians like *Eryops* and *Cycops*, and the sail-backed reptile *Dimetrodon*. There are also mammoth and mastodon fossils and a good *Glyptodon*, a huge ancestor of today's Texas armadillo.

Unfortunately, this museum has been seriously underfunded for years, and simply does not have the space or money to properly display its collection. To make matters worse, flooding early in 1990 damaged part of the Paleontology Hall, and repairs have been slow. This museum is a badly neglected treasure.

Oklahoma Museum of Natural History

Where: On the campus of the University of Oklahoma, 1335 Asp Avenue, Norman, OK 73019-0606

Hours: Tuesday through Friday, 10:00 A.M.-5:00 P.M.; weekends 2:00 P.M.-5:00 P.M. On home football game Saturdays, hours are 9:00 A.M.-1:00 P.M. Closed Monday.

Phone: (405) 325-4712

There are some important dinosaurs on display here; a baby *Brontosaurus* is of unusual interest. During the 1930s the university's Dr. J. Willis Stovall heard of exciting dinosaur discoveries made during road building near Kenton, Oklahoma, in western Cimarron County. Stovall immediately launched a dinosaur hunt of unusual scope. This was during the Great Depression and Professor Stovall was able to get help from the Works Progress Administration (WPA) in Washington. From 1935 to 1942 an estimated 10,000 bones were sent back to Norman. Many of them are now on exhibit in the museum.

But what this museum is really noted for is an exceptional display of prehistoric mammals. There are, of course, the familiar stars—a mammoth, a giant bison, a giant ground sloth, and *Smilodon fatalis*, largest of the saber-toothed cats. There are some rare specimens, that the visitor should be sure to seek out, even though they are not among the larger or flashier displays. There is, for example, *Epigaulus hatcheri*, a beaverlike rodent with horns. This creature was well adapted for digging, and the horns may have been used to help break up the soil. Along with the horned rodent, there is *Caenopus occidentalea*, a rhinoceros without a horn. There are extinct camels, tapirs, and a number of creatures which have no close living relatives today. Dog fossils are rare, but this collection has the lower jaw of what is called a "bone-eating dog." The teeth are very large, indicating that it was capable of crushing the bones of other animals. It probably lived the lifestyle of a predator/scavenger, much like the modern hyena. One of the great pleasures of visiting different museums is that it gives the visitor a greater sense of the enormous diversity of life in the ancient world.

Dinosaur Quarries

Where: Near Kenton, Oklahoma. For directions contact Bonnie Heppard, Box 36, Kenton, OK 73946
Phone: (405) 261-7474

During the 1930s several fossil quarries were excavated in the vicinity of Kenton in Cimarron County, Oklahoma. Some yielded the bones of Ice Age mammals, others the bones of dinosaurs, including *Brontosaurus*. A huge concrete replica of the femur of a *Brontosaurus* has been erected on the site at which a particularly fine specimen was found. Dinosaur tracks have also been found in the same area. The quarries and the tracks are on private land, but the owners are usually happy to let visitors see them. Bonnie Heppard, who runs a store in Kenton and is also postmistress, is the best local source of information.

NEW MEXICO

New Mexico Museum of Natural History

Where: 1801 Mountain Road N.W., Albuquerque, NM
               87104. Located in Old Town Albuquerque.
Hours: Open daily 9:00 A.M.-5:00 P.M.
Admission: Adults $4; Children over 12, Seniors, and Students $3.
               Children 3 to 11 years $1. There are additional fees
               for special exhibits and shows.
Phone: (505) 841-8837

What makes this state-of-the-art museum unique is that it's new, built during the 1980s. Most natural history museums have to fit their exhibits into buildings as much as a century old, and designed for old-style displays. Here the concept of the exhibit existed before the building went up, and the structure was designed to accommodate it. The theme of the museum is "Timetracks," a journey through several billion years of southwestern natural history. A visitor can walk through the exhibits or ride the Evolator, a word combining "elevator" and "evolution." Throughout the six-minute ride the Evolator vibrates and rumbles, scene after scene is flashed on multiple video screens, and portholes allow the visitor to look out over displays from various eras.

Naturally, it is the display from the Age of Dinosaurs that attracts the most attention. A very realistic model of a mother *Parasaurolophus*, one of the duck-billed dinosaurs, grazes among the trees and plants, keeping a careful eye on her offspring. In other parts of the exhibit there are models of *Stegosaurus* and *Camarasaurus* and, gliding above them is *Quetzalcoatlus*, a pterosaur that is the largest-known flying creature. Visitors can stand next to *Coelophysis*, New Mexico's state fossil, and gaze up at a 25-foot *Brachiosaurus* leg.

At the entrance to the museum stand two wonderful bronze dinosaurs created by New Mexico sculptor David A. Thomas. They are *Pentaceratops sternbergii* (popularly called Spike), a relative of the familiar *Triceratops*, and a 30-foot-long *Albertosaurus* which appears to be attacking Spike. Spike, who was installed in 1985, has been a particular favorite. His nose, horns, back, and tail have been worn shiny by the hundreds of children who climb on him daily.

And there's lots more, like an Ice Age cave, and a large saltwater aquarium with lots of sharks. At one time, largely arid New Mexico was a seacoast. A laser graphics display re-creates the life of a dinosaur from a fossil embedded in rock. The fossil is transformed into a moving figure that stands up and runs, catches an insect, gets into a fight with another dinosaur, is killed and transformed into the fossil that the display began with.

This museum draws its inspiration as much from theme parks like Disney World as from traditional natural history museums. Many of the exhibits were designed, at least in part, by a California firm founded by a couple of former Disney employees. Some of the innovations are disturbing to museum purists, but visitors to the New Mexico Museum of Natural History love them.

David A. Thomas, Sculptor

Where: 305 Alcazar N.E., Albuquerque, NM 87110
Phone: (505) 883-8061

David Thomas was a cartoonist and commercial artist who turned to sculpture in the 1960s. He had always been interested

in geology and paleontology, and this led him naturally to dinosaur sculpture. Today his incredibly lifelike sculptures can be found at the New Mexico Museum of Natural History, the Museum of the Rockies in Bozeman, Montana, and other places, mainly in the West. Accuracy is his first priority. "I will work at the point where science and art meet, and I am as dedicated to scientific accuracy as I am to creating a dynamic work of art. In photographs, my pieces look like living animals, not statues," he says. And he's right. They do look alive.

Thomas is an extremely friendly fellow who loves to talk about his work. Write or call; you'll get an answer. He is also more than happy to show off his work in progress if he happens to have something in his studio, and he has the time. But don't just drop in. Make an appointment.

Ruth Hall Museum
of Paleontology

Where: At the Ghost Ranch Conference Center, Abiquiu, NM
          87510
Phone: (505) 685-4333

In 1947 Dr. Edwin H. Colbert of the American Museum of
Natural History discovered what turned out to be a mass burial
site for dinosaurs, on a steep hillside at Ghost Ranch in New
Mexico. The species he found there was *Coelophysis*, a small
predatory dinosaur that lived about 195 million years ago,
making it one of the oldest-known dinosaurs ever found. The
remains of hundreds and hundreds of these creatures have
been excavated from this remarkable site. Complete dinosaur
skeletons of any kind are rare, but at Ghost Ranch at least one
hundred complete skeletons, with virtually all the bones in
articulation, have been discovered. Scientists can study a complete population, from chicken-sized babies to ostrich-sized
adults. All of these creatures seem to have died and been buried
at one time. Why, is a question that still puzzles scientists.

  Coelophysis fossils from Ghost Ranch can be found in museums all over the country, and excavations are still going on.
The little dinosaur has become the state fossil of New Mexico.
Ghost Ranch is now owned by the Presbyterian Church and
used as a conference and study center. The church has established a museum of anthropology and, more recently, a museum of paleontology at Ghost Ranch. The centerpiece of the
exhibit is a large block of fossil-bearing rock. When technicians
are at work, visitors are able to watch them at the delicate job
of removing the bones from the encasing matrix. The dinosaur
quarry itself is protected by the U.S. Department of the Interior
as a National Natural Landmark.

  While open to the public, the museum is primarily for

people staying at the conference center, so if you wish to visit it is wise to call ahead. Free-lance fossil hunting is absolutely forbidden.

Clayton Lake State Park

Where: About 12 miles north of Clayton, NM, off Highway 370.
Phone: (505) 374-8808

Dinosaur tracks in this park were first discovered in 1982, but the discovery did not come to the attention of park officials until people were observed trying to dig up the tracks and carry them away. More than 500 tracks have been found, most in hard stone where they are resistant to vandals and unauthorized collectors. Others are so fragile and, in some cases, so rare that those who know their locations are sworn to secrecy in order to protect them.

At least two sets of tracks are quite exceptional. One is a set of handprints from a pterodactyl, a flying reptile. Another is a set of prints left by a web-footed dinosaur that is otherwise unknown. The tracks open for public viewing are located about one-half mile from the parking lot near the lake. The trail leads over the dam. The best time to view the tracks is early in the morning or late in the afternoon. There is a walkway around the tracks with explanatory signs.

The Chamber of Commerce of the nearby town of Clayton has caught dinosaur fever. A model *Brontosaurus* (called Moonbeam) and a *Triceratops* (called Spike) are on display in front of the Tourist Information Office on South First Street. The town also has a *Tyrannosaurus rex* model (Raunchy Rex), who appears at parades and may be found in front of various businesses in town.

Petrified Forest
National Park

Where: On I-40 between Holbrook and Navajo, AZ. Mailing address, Petrified Forest National Park, AZ 86026
Phone: (602) 524-6228

This national park contains some of the strangest and most beautiful ancient artifacts in North America, indeed in the entire world. The formation of the petrified forest began some 225 million years ago during the late Triassic period or the beginning of the Age of Dinosaurs. At that time northeastern Arizona was a lush floodplain, where tall trees similar to modern sequoias and pine trees grew. As the trees died and fell into the marshy ground they were covered with silt, mud, and volcanic ash. This layer cut off oxygen and slowed decay. Gradually, water carrying silica from the volcanic ash seeped into the logs and, bit by bit, replaced the original wood tissue with silica deposits. As the process continued, the silicas hardened and the logs were preserved as petrified wood. In more recent geological time, wind and water wore away the accumulated layers of sediments, and exposed the petrified logs on the land's surface. Petrified wood is found in almost every state and in many countries, but Petrified Forest National Park has the largest-known concentration of petrified wood in the world. Here the fossilized trees are much older than most, and the petrified wood is more colorful.

The ancient Indians made tools and arrowheads from the material. They even built some of their homes with it, and traded it for shells and other special objects that were not found in the region. By the early 1900s pieces of petrified wood were being sold for jewelry and souvenirs. There was genuine concern that this unique place would be destroyed. In 1906 the area was established as a National Monument. Later, a portion of the Painted Desert was added and in 1962 it was declared a National Park.

Some fossil animals have been found, along with the petrified wood. In 1985 a large portion of the skeleton of a 20-foot-long ancient crocodile-like reptile, a phytosaur, was discovered just a few miles from the park's Painted Desert Visitor Center. The restored specimen will be put on display at the park. Since the Petrified Forest dates from the time when dinosaurs were just beginning to appear, fossils of some of the earliest dinosaurs have been found there. Some are on display at the park's Visitor Center or Rainbow Forest Museum, along with fossil fish and other creatures. But it's the giant petrified logs and breathtaking scenery that people, quite properly, come to see.

Museum of Northern Arizona

Where:　　Route 180 north of Flagstaff, AZ. Follow signs for Grand Canyon. Better still, call for directions. Mailing address, Route 4, Box 720, Flagstaff, AZ 86001

Hours:　　Daily 9:00 A.M.-5:00 P.M. Closed Thanksgiving, Christmas, and New Year's Day.

Admission: There is a nominal fee.

Phone:　　(602) 774-5211

The geology section of this extremely attractive regional museum is being completely redesigned, and is scheduled to be finished sometime in 1992. The new exhibit will have full-mounted skeletons of some small dinosaurs found in the region, dinosaur tracks, and a more impressive display of fossil mammals also from the region.

Arizona Museum of Science and Technology

Where: 80 North Street (southwest corner of Second Street and Adams Street) Phoenix, AZ 85004
Hours: Monday through Saturday, 9:00 A.M.-5:00 P.M.; Sunday, noon-5:00 P.M.
Admission: Adults $3.50; Children 4 through 12 years, and Seniors, $2.50; Children under 4 years free.
Phone: (602) 256-9388

The wide range of science and technology exhibits found in this museum include two life-size dinosaur skull casts, *Tyrannosaurus* and *Triceratops*, plus information on eight other dinosaurs. There is a good gift shop, and a first-rate ice-cream stand in the museum.

Rocky Mountains and Northern Great Plains

COLORADO

Dinosaur Valley

Where: 362 Main Street, Grand Junction, CO 81501
Hours: Memorial Day to September 30, 9:00 A.M.-5:00 P.M.,
               open to 7:00 P.M. Wednesday and Saturday. Winter
               hours, 10:00 A.M.-4:30 P.M. Tuesday through Sunday.
Admission: Adults $3.50; Children 2 to 12 years $2.
Phone: (303) 243-DINO (243-3466)

Operated by the Museum of Western Colorado, this exhibit devoted entirely to dinosaurs features a permanent display of Dinamation robotic dinosaurs. There are also lots of real fossils, many found in western Colorado. The most impressive single item may be a seven-foot-long *Brachiosaurus* femur. The facility contains a working paleontological laboratory where visitors can watch fossils being prepared for display and study.

Rabbit Valley Quarry

Where: Thirty miles west of Grand Junction, CO. Take the Rabbit
           Valley Exit on 1-70.
Hours: Open daily
Phone: (303) 241-9210

What has been called the "Trail Through Time" is a moderately strenuous one-and-a-half-mile walk through an area that has yielded many valuable dinosaur fossils. The well-marked, self-guided tour takes visitors past a *Camarasaurus* fossil. Limb bones and eighteen articulated vertebrates are visible in the rock. At another location the ribs, pelvis, and femur bones of *Diplodocus* can be seen. There are plant fossils, the location where the world's oldest *Iguanodon* was found, and much more. This is a place to find out what dinosaur fossils look like when they are found. The hike is a wonderful experience. Visitors should be warned that in the summer it can be unbearably hot and dry, and during May and June the gnats are fierce. Any discomfort is worth it, though.

Riggs Hill

Where: Take Highway 340 west from Grand Junction, CO, to South Broadway. Site located at the intersection of Meadows Way.
Hours: Open year round
Phone: Call Dinosaur Valley (303) 241-9210

In 1900 Elmer S. Riggs of the Field Museum of Chicago excavated the fossil remains of a *Brachiosaurus*, then believed to be the world's largest dinosaur. This is where the discovery was made. A well-marked trail through this important site is about three-quarters of a mile long.

Garden Park Fossil Area

Where: About eight miles north of Canyon City, CO, on county Highway 9. *State* highway 9 also runs north from Canyon City. Don't get them mixed up.
Hours: Open daily
Phone: (719) 275-2331 for information on tours of Garden Park area and other activities.

Historically, this was one of the most significant Jurassic dinosaur sites in America. Edward Drinker Cope and Othniel

Charles Marsh, the two great fossil hunting rivals, both had teams working here in the 1870s. Though the glory days for collecting at Garden Park are probably over, some discoveries are still being made, and there is a potential for additional important discoveries. A roadside marker indicates the location of the site.

Dinosaur Hill

Where: On Highway 340, one and one-half miles south of the city of Fruita, CO.
Hours: Open daily
Phone: Call Dinosaur Valley (303) 241-9210

Visitors can take a 45-minute hike through an historic site where many important dinosaur finds were made earlier in the century. The trail is well marked.

Denver Museum of Natural History

Where: 2001 Colorado Boulevard, Denver, CO 80205-5798
Hours: Daily 9:00 A.M.-5:00 P.M. Closed Christmas Day.
Admission: Adults $4; Children 4 to 12 years, and Seniors, $2; Children under 4 years free
Phone: (303) 322-7009

There are a number of "open" fossil laboratories, where visitors can watch specimens being prepared for display. This museum has one of the best, because it uses state-of-the-art technology to extract and prepare the specimens. The lab will show visitors how skeletons are put together, as well as how they are studied with modern computers and equipment. There is also an area for the preparation of small fossils, minute traces of prehistoric organisms that usually are not very interesting to look at but, scientifically, are extremely important. Visitors will be able to discover every facet of these tiny fossils as scientists study them under a microscope, with special video connections to a large color monitor. Computer models of the specimen may also be used to enhance the picture visitors will see.

The museum is planning a major expansion of its prehistoric life exhibits. In the meantime, there are still four excellent dinosaur skeletons on display, plus a large collection of prehistoric mammals.

Dino Productions

Where: P.O. Box 3004, Englewood, CO 80155-3004
Phone: (303) 741-1587

Jan and John Jerkins, a couple of academically trained geologists who "became oil and gas company orphans in 1986," founded this mail-order house that specializes in earth science materials for home and classroom. Though their carefully prepared catalog contains materials related to many areas of science, paleontology and particularly dinosaurs are fully represented. Aside from the familiar selection of books and games, there are some really unique items. There are high-quality and reasonably priced fossil replicas. An *Albertosaurus* tooth costs $4.00, a *Triceratops* toe bone $4.50. Each is accompanied by a detailed information card. There are dinosaur models, from a small mass-produced *Allosaurus* for $4.65, to a large handmade cast of *Stegosaurus* for $825. Particularly useful are the maps "Pathway to the Dinosaurs," geologic highway maps loaded with information about where people can visit various types of dinosaur displays and sites. There is one map for Colorado, Wyoming, and Utah, and a second for Texas. The company also sponsors "dinosaur safaris," guided tours of Rocky Mountain dinosaur sites. Get a catalog. You're sure to find something you want, probably lots of things.

UTAH

Dinosaur National Monument

Where: Take U.S. Highway 40 to Jensen, UT, then follow
                    Utah Highway 149 north for three miles to the Di-
                    nosaur Quarry Visitor Center. Mailing address, P.O.
                    Box 210, Dinosaur, CO 81610

Hours: Open 8:00 A.M.-5:00 P.M. every day except Christmas,
                    New Year's Day, and Thanksgiving. Open until 7:00
                    P.M. during the summer. Parking is limited during the
                    summer, so visitors may have to go to the main parking
                    area and take a shuttlebus to the Quarry building.

Admission: There is a $5 per vehicle entrance fee at the Dinosaur
                    Quarry entrance, good for seven consecutive days.
                    There are also fees for the use of some campgrounds.
                    A variety of different passes for frequent visitors and
                    senior citizens are available.

Phone: For information about the entire area call Dinosaurland
                    Travel Board (800) 477-5558 or (801) 789-1352.

An area bounded by Vernal, Utah; Price, Utah; and Grand
Junction, Colorado, is known as the Dinosaur Triangle, because there are so many fossil sites and other dinosaur-related
attractions. The most popular site in the Dinosaur Triangle,
indeed one of the most significant dinosaur fossil sites in North
America, is in Dinosaur National Monument.

This is a large park with many attractions—camping, ca-
noeing, fishing, and hiking—amid magnificent Western scenery. It spans two states and has several entrances. Therefore,
it is important for the visitor to know that there is only one
spot in the park where visitors can see dinosaur bones, that is,
at the Quarry. A building covers the 200-foot face of a rock

wall in which a huge number of dinosaur bones are embedded. The bones here are not removed except under unusual circumstances. Instead, they are "reliefed"—as much rock as possible is removed from around the bones so that they are easily visible. Today, visitors to the Quarry can see more than 2,000 bones exposed on the Quarry face. Work in the Quarry usually begins in mid-April when temperatures reach a comfortable level, and stops at the beginning of November. Along the Quarry wall *Brontosaurus*, *Stegosaurus*, *Camarasaurus*, *Allosaurus*, and *Camptosaurus* bones are all visible from the visitors' platform. There is nothing like this anywhere else in the world.

Exhibits and displays help explain the lives of the dinosaurs, and how this particularly rich fossil-bearing area was formed. There are tours and special programs as well. Check the bulletin board, or ask the Rangers; they are knowledgeable and exceptionally helpful.

Utah Field House of Natural History and Dinosaur Gardens

Where: These two attractions are next to one another on East
             Main Street in Vernal, UT 84078
Hours: The Field House is open 8:00 A.M.-9:00 P.M. during
             the summer. Winter hours are 9:00 A.M.-5:00 P.M.
             Closed Thanksgiving, Christmas, and New Year's Day.
             The Gardens are entered through the Field House.
Admission: Adults $1; Children 6 to 16 years .50¢. Car load, up
             to eight persons, $3.
Phone: (801) 789-3799

The Field House, which is the museum part of this dual exhibit, has bones of *Stegosaurus, Camarasaurus, Diplodocus,* and other fossils, as well as exhibits which depict the area from the prehistoric to present times. Dinosaur Gardens is a showcase for fourteen fiberglass and polyester, life-size models of prehistoric creatures, most of them dinosaurs. The models were made by sculptor Elbert Porter and purchased by the state of Utah in 1977. It took some years to find a proper place to display the giant creatures. When the Field House was being remodeled a decision was made to build a suitable habitat for the models next door. The Gardens feature a small lake, a swamp area, and a simulated rock outcropping with a bridge and waterfall. Existing trees and shrubs have been cultivated to resemble foliage from the time of the dinosaurs. Visitors stroll past an 80-foot-long *Diplodocus* and a 30-foot *Triceratops. Tyrannosaurus rex* towers twenty feet above the walkway. An excellent lighting system makes this attraction a lot of fun to visit at night. In December the dinosaurs are hung with thousands of Christmas lights. It's quite a sight.

Cleveland-Lloyd
Dinosaur Quarry

Where: Thirty miles south of Price, UT, on Highway 10. Follow
signs to the Quarry. Mailing address, P.O. Drawer A.B.,
Price, UT 84501.
Hours: Thursday through Monday, 10:00 A.M.-5:00 P.M. Memo-
rial Day through Labor Day. Open weekends Easter until
Memorial Day.
Phone: (801) 637-4584

Though the area is dry and hilly now, 147 million years ago
it was a shallow lake. Dinosaurs were attracted to the lush
vegetation, and became trapped in the mud, where they made
easy prey for meat-eating dinosaurs. Over 18,000 dinosaur
bones have been removed from this quarry, representing ten
different species. Three-quarters of the bones recovered are
from *Allosaurus.* The site was designated a registered National
Natural Landmark in 1966. There is a Visitor Center with
displays, excellent views of the quarry itself, and a nature trail.

College of Eastern Utah
Prehistoric Museum

Where: At the rear of the Municipal Building, Price, UT 84501
Hours: Monday through Saturday 9:00 A.M.-5:00 P.M.
Phone: (801) 637-5060

The most imposing dinosaur in this museum is Al the *Allosaurus,* the museum's mascot and state fossil of Utah. This
skeleton came from the Cleveland-Lloyd Dinosaur Quarry,
about thirty miles away. Other dinosaur displays include a
Stegosaurus skeleton, purchased by contributions to a "Buy a
Bone" campaign. An unusual display is a large collection of
dinosaur footprints, most of them taken from the ceilings of

nearby coal mines by local resident Robert Rowley. The museum has ambitious plans for future expansion and one day hopes to house a dozen complete dinosaur skeletons.

Robert Rowley, Dinosaur Tracks

Where: 305 South 100 East, Price, UT 84501
Phone: (801) 637-2340

Millions of years ago dinosaurs went stomping around the swamps, and left their footprints deep in the surfaces. These footprint depressions were filled with mud, silt, and sand. Eventually the vegetation that had fallen into the swamp turned to coal. When the coal was mined, impressions of these ancient dinosaur footprints could be found in the roofs of mines. Robert Rowley, a former coal miner who also studied geology, has spent years examining and collecting dinosaur footprints from mines. Many of these come from the Price River Coal Company mine in Spring Canyon, west of Helper, Utah.

The dinosaur prints are found in mine roof surfaces as sandstone protrusions which hang down from the roof, sometimes as much as twelve inches. Rowley believes he has the largest collection of what he calls "Natural Cast" dinosaur footprints in the world. He has donated many of these prints to museums throughout the United States where they are now on display. He also makes polyester casts of original prints that are sold at museum gift shops and schools. Or they can be ordered directly from Rowley himself. Write to him for more information. He is very proud of the collecting he has done, and more than willing to share information.

Emery County Museum

Where: In the Castle Dale, UT, City Hall on First Street, one
             block north of Main Street
Hours: Monday through Friday, 9:00 A.M.-5:00 P.M.; Satur-
             day, 10:00 A.M.-5:00 P.M. Closed Sunday, Christmas,
             Thanksgiving, and 4th of July.
Admission: Suggested donation $1.
Phone: (801) 381-5252

A local history museum, but since so many dinosaur fossils
have been found in the area, they are very definitely part of
the local history. There is a replica skeleton of *Allosaurus* from
the nearby Cleveland-Lloyd Dinosaur Quarry. A new facility
is being built, so it is best for visitors to phone ahead to see
what is open.

Utah Museum of Natural History

Where: At the President's Circle on the University of Utah
             campus, Salt Lake City, UT 84112
Hours: Monday through Saturday, 9:30 A.M.-5:30 P.M.; Sun-
             day, noon-5:00 P.M. Closed July 4, July 24, Thanks-
             giving, Christmas, and New Year's Day.
Admission: Adults $2; Children and Seniors $1
Phone: (801) 581-4303

Utah dinosaur quarries were the source for several excellent
mounted skeletons in this collection. They include *Allosaurus*,
Barosaurus, *Camptosaurus*, and *Stegosaurus*. There are also
lots of smaller fossils. What is unusual for this dinosaur-laden
state is that the museum has an excellent collection of Ice Age
fossils. The prize of the second floor fossil mammal exhibit is

a cast of the best-preserved and most-complete skeleton of the Columbian mammoth ever found. The bones were discovered in August, 1988, in the mountains of central Utah.

Earth Sciences Museum

Where: On the campus of Brigham Young University, 1683 North Canyon Road, Provo, UT 84602
Hours: Monday, 8:00 A.M.-9:00 P.M.; Tuesday through Friday, 8:00 A.M.-5:00 P.M.; Saturday, 10:00 A.M.-5:00 P.M. Closed Sundays and major holidays.
Phone: (801) 378-2232

This small museum has displays on two of the largest known dinosaurs, *Ultrasaurus* and *Supersaurus*. There is also a 150 million-year-old dinosaur egg. X-rays of the egg show what scientists believe to be a fossilized dinosaur embryo. There is a window into the museum's paleontological laboratory, which allows visitors to see the scientists and technicians at work. The museum has a large and important collection of dinosaur fossils which are not on display, simply because the building is so small. The staff is currently engag d in a strenuous effort to raise money for a larger facility.

Mill Canyon Dinosaur Trail

Where: About 13 miles from Moab, UT, on Highway 191. Turn off at Highway Mile Marker No 141 and follow the signs.
Hours: Open daily

There is a self-guided quarter-mile trail through this very interesting site. The visitor passes rocks containing bones from a variety of dinosaurs. A detailed brochure, available at the start of the trail, explains what can be seen. The Dinosaur Trail is described as a bold experiment—an outdoor paleontological museum. There are no guards or fences, and many of the fossils are fragile and easily damaged. In fact, there is a special display of a vandalized bone, compared with bones prepared in place by experienced paleontologists. Removing or destroying anything from fossils to plants is strictly illegal here, as it is in all other major fossil sites.

Warner Valley Dinosaur Tracksite

Where: c/o Dixie Resource Area, Bureau of Land Management, 225 Bluff Street, St. George, UT 84770
Hours: Open year round, weather permitting.
Phone: (801) 673-4654

The trackways from two different types of dinosaurs may be seen at this site, which is located in Warner Valley, southwest of St. George, Utah. This dirt road is a Utah Travel Council "Scenic Backway" which also takes the traveler to the historic site of Fort Pierce. The road is impassable when wet. The route has signs, but it is not easy to find, so it is advisable to contact the Bureau of Land Management office in St. George for specific directions. A short trail leads to the trackways and an information sign.

Dan O'Laurie Museum

Where: 118 East Center Street in downtown Moab, UT 84532
Hours: May 1 to September 30, 1:00 P.M.-5:00 P.M. and 7:00 P.M.-9:00 P.M. daily. October 1 to April 30, Monday through Thursday, 3:00 P.M.-5:00 P.M. and 7:00 P.M.-9:00 P.M. Friday and Saturday, 1:00 P.M.-5:00 P.M. and 7:00 P.M.-9:00 P.M. Closed Sunday, New Year's Day, Christmas Day, July 4th, and Thanksgiving.
Phone: (801) 259-7985

Many local history museums in dinosaur country have some dinosaur fossils on display, and this one in Moab is no exception. There are some good dinosaur footprints.

Weber State College
Museum of Natural Science

Where: In the Lind Lecture Hall on the campus of Weber State
College, 3705 Harrison Boulevard, Ogden, UT 84408
Hours: Monday through Friday, 8:00 A.M.-4:00 P.M.
Phone: (801) 626-6653

The exhibit includes a replica of *Allosaurus* and *Brontosaurus*
bones. There is also the sail-backed reptile *Dimetrodon*, which
is not a dinosaur, but quite impressive anyway, and some early
mammals.

Dinosaur Bone Cabin

Where: On U.S. Highway 30, between Medicine Bow and Rock
River, WY, at the county line
Hours: The cabin is there, but may not always be open.

Dinosaur bones were so numerous in this area that in the mid-nineteenth century an unknown sheepherder used them to make the foundation of his cabin. Perhaps he thought they were just oddly shaped rocks. A replica of the sheepherder's cabin stands southeast of Medicine Bow. A number of historically important dinosaur fossil quarries are located nearby, and a roadside marker describes what you are seeing. You might not want to enter the cabin, even if it is open. Like many rocks in this area, the bones are impregnated with uranium and are radioactive!

University of Wyoming Geological Museum

Where: S.H. Knight Geology Building, University of Wyoming campus. Mailing address, P.O. Box 3006, Laramie, WY 82071-3006.
Hours: 8:00 A.M.-5:00 P.M. weekdays. Occasional weekends 10:00 A.M.-1:00 P.M. Closed holidays.
Phone: (307) 766-4218 or 766-3386

Dr. S.H. Knight, a University of Wyoming geologist, spent his spare time hammering copper sheets into a life-sized reconstruction of *Tyrannosaurus rex.* The copper dinosaur now

guards the front entrance of the building which bears Knight's name and houses Wyoming's best collection of dinosaur fossils. Just inside the front door is a complete skeleton of *Apatosaurus* (or *Brontosaurus*) that stretches the entire length of the museum. It is one of only five such skeletons in the world. There is a fine *Triceratops* skull and other material from familiar dinosaurs. Recently the skeleton of a juvenile *Maiasaura*, no more than a year old, has been put on display in the balcony. This is the dinosaur known for building nests, and there is a nearby display of dinosaur eggs and nests. Another new display allows visitors to feel a cast of fossilized dinosaur skin.

The artistically talented Dr. Knight also did a couple of murals of ancient life in Wyoming, which are hung in the museum.

SOUTH DAKOTA

Dinosaur Park

Where: Skyline Drive, west off Quincy Street, Rapid City, SD.
Hours: Open year round. Dinosaurs are lighted until 10:00 P.M.
Concessions closed in the winter.

During the Great Depression of the 1930s the Works Project
Administration (WPA) created seven life-sized concrete replicas of dinosaurs on a hill in Rapid City. The largest of these,
the *Brontosaurus*, is visible from most points in the city. These
models were not particularly accurate when they were built,
and are even less so today. But they are very solid, have been
well maintained, and make terrific photographs. They are
painted a vivid green. Kids love climbing all over the models,
which are surrounded by sand, so they don't get hurt falling
off. These are also the oldest surviving outdoor dinosaur

models in the United States, and thus have some historic significance as well. Local tourist officials say that Dinosaur Park attracts as many visitors as the nearby, and far more famous, Mount Rushmore.

Museum of Geology

Where: The second floor of the O'Hara Building, 500 East St. Joseph Street, on the campus of the South Dakota School of Mines and Technology, Rapid City, SD.

Hours: Memorial Day to Labor Day, Monday through Saturday, 8:00 A.M.-6:00 P.M.; Sunday, noon-6:00 P.M. After Labor Day until Memorial Day, Monday through Friday, 8:00 A.M.-5:00 P.M.; Saturday, 9:00 A.M.-2:00 P.M.; Sunday, 2:00 P.M.-4:00 P.M. Closed major holidays.

Phone: (605) 394-2467

It's a bit surprising to find that the most impressive skeletons in this excellent little museum are those of marine reptiles like a plesiosaur and a mosasaur. But at one time much of what is now South Dakota was covered by the vast inland sea in which these creatures lived. There are dinosaurs as well. Rising majestically to overlook the entire collection is a complete duck-billed *Edmontosaurus*, from Custer County. This is the most common type of dinosaur found in South Dakota. No one can pass the huge *Tyrannosaurus* skull without at least a little shiver of fear. The skull was found in Butte County. The nearby Badlands have been a rich source of fossils from the Age of Mammals, and the museum contains the best exhibit of Badlands fossils to be found anywhere. There are saber-toothed cats, giant pigs, titanotheres, and lots more. Visitors to this popular tourist area should be sure to put aside some time for a visit to the Museum of Geology. They won't be disappointed.

The Mammoth Site

Where: Hot Springs, SD, one block north of the Highway 18 truck bypass. Mailing address, P.O. Box 606, Hot Springs, SD 57747

Hours: Open year round. Hours vary by season.

Admission: Adults $3.95; Seniors $3.50; Children 6 to 12 years $1.95. Tax is added to each admission. Children under 5 years free.

Phone: (605) 745-6017

Some 26,000 years ago 10-ton Columbian mammoths came to a particularly steep-sided water hole in what is now Hot Springs, South Dakota. Many of them either slipped or waded into the pool, were trapped, and died there. This went on for about 500 years until the watering hole eventually filled up with earth, leaving an immense concentration of the bones of mammoths and other animals of that era. In 1974 a heavy equipment operator leveling ground for a housing development uncovered something unusual, a tusk about seven feet long, and nearby were a profusion of bones. Excavation for the housing stopped, and the process of excavating the great mammoth graveyard began.

A million-dollar Visitor Center has now been built over the site. Walkways allow visitors to get a firsthand, closeup look at ongoing excavations. The work is extremely delicate and painstaking, for mammoth bones, unlike the far older dinosaur bones, are fragile and easily damaged by careless digging.

This is a spectacular excavation, the only in situ (bones left as found) display of mammoth fossils in America, and perhaps the largest anywhere in the world. The remains of at least 42 mammoths have been uncovered so far, and scientists believe that there may be as many as 100. The remains of other animals, like *Arctodus simus*, the giant short-faced bear that was possibly the most powerful predator of the Ice Age, an extinct camel, and more familiar animals like the gray wolf have also been found.

When the weather is right, a small army of volunteers and scientists dig, chisel, scrape, pick, and brush their way into the mass of bones with infinite patience. While the work goes on, care is taken to expose and vividly display the bones in the ground. The nonprofit organization that manages the site hopes that one day it can be developed into a major center specializing in research of fossil elephants. In the meantime it has been attracting 50,000 visitors a year. Explanations of the significance of the work that is going on are complete and well presented. The Mammoth Site is both visually stunning, and highly informative. It is not to be missed.

Flintstones Bedrock City

Where: At the intersection of U.S. Highways 16 and 385, Custer, SD. Mailing address, Box 649, Custer, SD 57730
Hours: Open early May through mid-September.
Phone: (605) 673-4079 Out-of-state calls for information on the Custer area (800) 992-9818

Anyone touring the magnificent scenic attractions of South Dakota might want to stop off at Flintstones Bedrock City for a Brontoburger or a Dino Dog. This is a combination campground and amusement park, with such attractions as Mount Rockmore and twenty "stone age" buildings and shops. The kids can be photographed in front of Fred Flintstone's house. Fred himself might get in the picture. And you can fill your gas tank at the Texrocko Gas Station. It isn't Disneyland, but it's kind of unusual.

Wall Drug Dinosaur

Where: On Interstate 90 at Wall, South Dakota, 54 miles east of Rapid City. Mailing address, 510 Main Street, Wall, SD 57790.

Hours: The dinosaur is always there; the Drug Store is open most of the time.

Practically anywhere you go in the world you might find a sign or bumper sticker advertising Wall Drug Store in tiny Wall, South Dakota (population 800) at the entrance to the Badlands. It's more than a drug store, it's a restaurant, gas station, gift shop, museum, and monument to the power of aggressive promotion. For years the store's ebullient owner, Bill Hustead, has been giving out signs and bumper stickers promoting the family business. And it's worked! During the tourist season this country store has thousands of customers every day. At six in the morning the main street of Wall is crowded with the cars of people going for breakfast at Wall Drug, or just wanting to see the place. You can get a good and inexpensive breakfast, look at the stuffed elk heads, or be photographed with the statue of Cowboy Pete. The gigantic eighty-foot-long green-and-white *Brontosaurus*, standing by the roadside, is just another of Hustead's promotional gimmicks. You couldn't miss this place if you tried, and you shouldn't.

Leonard Hall Museum

Where: The geology building on the campus of the University of North Dakota. Mailing address, Box 8068, University Station, Grand Forks, ND 58202

Hours: Monday through Friday, 8:00 A.M.-4:30 P.M. Closed major holidays.

Admission: No regular charge, but donations are suggested.

Phone: (701) 777-2011

The lobby of the geology building contains a wide range of displays, including a dandy *Triceratops* skull that was found in 1963 near Marmarth, North Dakota. It is the only dinosaur material on display. On the outside of the building silhouette figures of *Brontosaurus* and *Triceratops* are embedded in the brick walls.

MONTANA

Museum of the Rockies

Where: On the south edge of the Montana State University campus, South 6th Street and Kagy Boulevard, Bozeman, MT 59717-0040

Hours: Memorial Day to Labor Day, 9:00 A.M.-9:00 P.M. daily. Winter hours: Tuesday through Saturday, 9:00 A.M.-5:00 P.M.; Sunday, 1:00 P.M.-5:00 P.M. Closed Monday, Thanksgiving, Christmas Day, New Year's Day.

Admission: Adults $3; Children 5 to 18 years $2; Family $10; Children under 5 years free.

Phone: (406) 994-2251

For many years important dinosaur finds made in Montana were shipped out of state, simply because there was no state museum equipped to properly display them. That all changed in 1978 when John R. Horner, who had made many important discoveries in Montana, left Princeton to devote his efforts to building up the Museum of the Rockies on the campus of Montana State University. A new building with a separate Hall of Dinosaurs, emphasizing Montana discoveries, was opened in 1989. This exhibit has been improved and expanded since the opening.

One of the most important discoveries made by Horner and his associates was a "nest" containing the remains of fifteen baby dinosaurs. As excavations continued, a dozen or so nests and 500 whole or partial dinosaur eggs were found. The place where the finds were made has been dubbed "Egg Gulch." Also found in the area were the bones of dinosaurs ranging in age from adult to "teen-age." This led to the conclusion that the dinosaurs laid their eggs in densely packed colonies and guarded them from predators. After the young were hatched, they were fed and protected until they were large enough to take care of themselves. Horner named the dinosaur that produced these eggs *Maiasaura*, "good mother reptile." This was one of the discoveries which helped to change today's perception of dinosaurs. An animal that could carefully care for its young was clearly not the brainless, lumbering pile of flesh that dinosaurs had once been thought to be. *Maiasaura* has been adopted as the state fossil of Montana, and specimens from this remarkable find form the centerpiece for this museum's dinosaur exhibit. But there's lots more.

Visitors to the museum are greeted by a roaring, growling robotic *Triceratops*. Three models of the gigantic pterosaur *Quetzalcoatlus* are suspended above models of *Maiasaura* tending her young. A few feet away a colony of small dinosaurs known as *Orodromeus* are shown in a nesting site in the middle of a large lake. One of the most exciting exhibits will be a virtually complete skeleton of *Tyrannosaurus rex*. This specimen, found in the vicinity of Hell Creek, Montana, is being prepared for display, and is expected to reveal new information about how the giant carnivore lived.

In 1956 this museum was housed in a Quonset hut on the Montana State University campus. It now has one of the most important dinosaur collections in the world, and state-of-the-art displays. There are also exhibits on the forebears of Native Americans, as well as on Montana's settlement and development within the past century. But this is truly a museum that dinosaurs built.

Be sure to ask at the museum for directions to places where excavations may be viewed in the field.

Carter County Museum

Where: 100 Main Street, Ekalaka, MT 59324
Hours: Tuesday through Friday, 9:00 A.M.-5:00 P.M. (closed one
hour at noon); Saturday and Sunday, 1:00 P.M.-5:00 P.M.
Closed Monday and major holidays.
Phone: (406) 775-6886

This is a small regional museum with some dinosaur skeletons which make many larger museums turn green with envy. There is a complete skeleton of the duck-billed dinosaur *Anatosaurus*, found just 35 miles west of Ekalaka. There is also an excellent *Triceratops* skull and a skull of the strange dome-headed *Pachycephalosaurus*. When visitors are finished exploring the museum they can drive ten miles north to Medicine Rocks State Park, and have a picnic in the midst of some of the strangest scenery in North America.

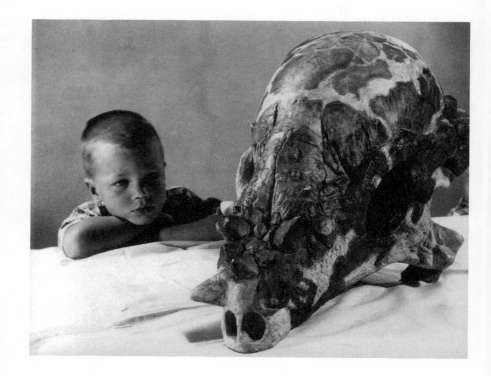

IDAHO

Idaho Museum of Natural History

Where: On the campus of Idaho State University. Mailing address, Box 8096, Pocatello, ID 83209-0009

Hours: Monday through Saturday, 9:00 A.M.-5:00 P.M.; Sunday, noon-5:00 P.M.

Admission: The museum is free, but there can be a charge for special exhibits.

Phone: (208) 236-3366 or 236-3168

A rotating special exhibit of Dinamation robotic dinosaurs and other prehistoric creatures will appear at the museum until 1993. Some of the figures will be changed regularly. Historically, few dinosaur fossils have been found in Idaho, and so not many are on display in this museum. However, there is an excellent collection of Ice Age mammal remains from the state's Snake River plain and elsewhere. The museum's collection of giant bison bones is the largest in the world.

West Coast

CALIFORNIA

San Diego Natural History Museum

Where: 1788 El Prado, Balboa Park, P.O. Box 1390, San Diego, CA 92112
Hours: Daily, 10:00 A.M.-4:30 P.M. (until 5:00 P.M. during the summer). Closed Thanksgiving, Christmas, and New Year's Day.
Admission: Adults $5; Children 6 to 18 years $1; Children 5 years and under free.
Phone: (619) 232-3821

California is not rich in dinosaur fossils. The only one ever found in San Diego County, an armor-plated *Nodosaurus*, can be found in this museum, along with a full *Allosaurus* reconstruction. Once visitors have seen the animals of the past in the museum, they can walk to the world-famous San Diego Zoo to view animals of the present.

Natural History Museum of Los Angeles County

Where: 900 Exposition Boulevard in Exposition Park, one block east of Vermont Avenue, Los Angeles, CA
Hours: Tuesday through Sunday, 10:00 A.M.-5:00 P.M. Closed Monday, Thanksgiving, Christmas, and New Year's Day.
Admission: Adults $3; Children 12 to 17 years and Seniors $1.50; Children 5 to 12 years .75¢; Children under 5 years free.
Phone: (213) 744-3414. Recorded message (213) 744-DINO (744-3466)

The collection of dinosaur fossils in this museum is not large, but what they have is excellent, and extremely popular. The dinosaur exhibits include a duck-billed dinosaur, *Camptosaurus*, the carnivorous *Allosaurus* posed as if in battle, and one of the finest *Tyrannosaurus rex* skulls on view anywhere. The collection of fossil mammals is far larger. The museum has many of the best fossils found in the famed La Brea Tar Pits. A saber-toothed cat is the institution's symbol. The museum, located at the Tar Pits themselves, is a satellite of the Natural History Museum. Among the activities offered in the new Discovery Center is the chance to make fossil rubbings from a realistic-looking rock wall. There is also a Dinosaur Shop offering T-shirts, models, and other dinosaur souvenirs and gifts.

George C. Page Museum
of La Brea Discoveries

Where: 5801 Wilshire Boulevard in Hancock Park, seven miles west of downtown Los Angeles, and two blocks east of Fairfax Avenue.

Hours: Tuesday through Sunday, 10:00 A.M.-5:00 P.M. Closed Monday, Thanksgiving Day, Christmas, and New Year's Day.

Admission: Adults $3; Seniors and Students $1.50; Children 12 to 5 years .75¢. Children under 5 years free. Parking is extra.

Phone: (213) 857-6311. Recorded information (213) 936-2230.

Rancho La Brea, once a Mexican land grant near the small Pueblo de los Angeles and now a park in the heart of America's second-largest city, is one of the world's most famous fossil sites. Tar pits formerly mined for natural asphalt have yielded the richest collection of Ice Age fossils that have been found anywhere in the world. No other site even comes close.

For tens of thousands of years asphalt seeped to the surface, particularly during warm summer weather. The shallow puddles were often concealed by a coating of dust and leaves. Unwary animals would become trapped in the sticky substance. Their struggles in turn lured carnivores and scavengers, such as saber-toothed cats, dire wolves, and huge condors. These were also trapped in the sticky material and perished along with their prey. The remains of an exceptionally large number of carnivores have been found here. Their bones became saturated with asphalt and sank into the pools. During the winter, cool temperatures solidified the asphalt, and streams deposited a layer of sediment over the exposed bones. The warm weather of early summer dried up the streams and liquefied the asphalt, resetting the trap. Approximately 420 different species of animals, from giant ground sloths and huge mammoths to tiny insects, have been recovered from the asphalt of Rancho La Brea. One human skeleton, about 9,000 years old, has also been found.

The asphalt deposits themselves have been used by man since prehistoric times, and the importance of the fossils was recognized just over a century ago. Fossils from the site were exhibited all over the world. Rancho La Brea was given to Los Angeles in 1916, but the museum was not completed there until 1977, and it has become a deservedly popular tourist attraction.

A visit to the museum begins with an introductory film on the history of the La Brea Tar Pits. Then there is a demonstration which graphically shows how sticky asphalt is, and how animals the size of a mammoth would be unable to escape its grasp. There are plenty of skeletons, including a display of the skulls of over 400 dire wolves.

Excavations are still going on, and there is a glass-walled paleontological laboratory that allows visitors to watch scientists and technicians at work cleaning, identifying, and cataloging new finds.

This is a famous, and not to be missed, attraction.

CALIFORNIA _____ 167

Knott's Berry Farm

Where:　　8039 Beach Boulevard (Highway 39) in Buena Park, CA, one-half mile south of the Riverside (91) freeway, twenty miles from downtown Los Angeles and six miles from Disneyland.

Hours:　　Open every day except Christmas. Operating hours vary, with extended hours during the summer months and holiday periods. Call (714) 220-5220 for exact hours.

Admission:　Adults $21; Children 3 through 11 years $16; Seniors (60 and over) $15. Prices are subject to change and there are some discount admissions available.

Phone:　　(714) 827-1776 for general information

This is one of America's most popular theme parks, with 165 rides and shows spread over 150 acres. The most spectacular adventure attraction at the park is a $7 million-dollar ride called Kingdom of the Dinosaurs. It begins in the Roaring '20s section of the park. Visitors board cars on a dock designed to resemble a Los Angeles trolley car station in the 1920s. The car takes a wrong turn into a mad scientist's laboratory where a time machine propels riders back in time. Beginning with glimpses of the Renaissance and the Byzantine eras, riders quickly emerge into the time of Early Man, complete with a cave man and woman. There is also a woolly mammoth, saber-toothed cat, and other prehistoric mammals. Then it's back to the time of the dinosaurs themselves, the high point of the trip. The roaring *Tyrannosaurus* and screeching *Pteranodon* always set the younger visitors screaming, and even provide a thrill for the older and more sophisticated.

The adventure ride takes eight minutes and features eleven dinosaurs, nine prehistoric mammals, and three human figures. The figures, created by California's Sequoia Creative, Inc., are all animated. Special effects for the attraction include

the chill of an Ice Age scene, the heat of an erupting volcano, crackling fires, sparkling time tunnels, a sky full of stars, a bubbling tar pit, and an aurora borealis in the night sky. A musical score was created especially for this attraction.

Amid the many shops in Knott's Berry Farm is the DinoStore/Discovery Center.

Prehistoric Journeys

Where: P.O. Box 3376, Santa Barbara, CA 93130
Phone: (805) 967-0074

You know that something costs more than you could possibly afford when the catalog doesn't even give you a price. The Prehistoric Journeys catalog offers a late Cretaceous *Triceratops* skull, 6½ feet long by 7 feet tall. Yes, a real fossil dinosaur skull, and a spectacular one at that. No price is given; just call for details. A much more common titanothere skull, advertised in the same catalog, was going for $7,500.

Not all this company's fossils have astronomical price tags. Fossil dinosaur tracks are available for under $100, and dinosaur teeth can be purchased for as little as $15. Then, there are coprolites—that's fossilized dinosaur dung—for $20. The buyer gets a certificate of authenticity with each purchase, and they are advertised as "A real conversation piece." There is even a mini-fossil collection for the beginning paleontologist.

Call or write for a catalog.

Skullduggery

Where: 621 South B Street, Tustin, CA 92680
Phone: 1-800-3-FOSSIL (1-800-336-7745) from 8:00 A.M. to 5:00
P.M. Pacific time.

Have you ever dreamed of owning your very own dinosaur skull? Sure you have; who hasn't? Then Skullduggery should be of interest to you. Since 1978 this California company has been producing and selling museum-quality replicas of fossils. A small-scale model (10 inches long) of a *Tyrannosaurus rex* skull sells for $99, plus shipping. A full-size model would be a little bulky for the average home, and ruinously expensive. This *Tyrannosaurus* skull, and many of the other items sold by Skullduggery, are not cheap, but they are accurate in every detail and are meant for serious collectors. A less expensive item is a full-size replica of a *Tyrannosaurus* tooth; it's 11 inches long and goes for $39.95.

While fossil models make up the bulk of this unique company's business, Skullduggery sells other interesting products —saber-toothed cat rings, *Tyrannosaurus* earrings, even a pocketknife with a handle made from fossilized *Brontosaurus* bone. The company assures us that all dinosaur bone used in the knives is from fragments unsuitable for scientific study.

You can visit the company's California showroom, but most of their business is mail-order, so call or write for a catalog.

Dinamation

Where: 27362 Calle Arroyo, San Juan Capistrano, CA 92675
Phone: (714) 493-7440

One of the most surprising business successes of the 1980s was a company that makes dinosaurs. The company is Dinamation, and it produces the most popular displays of robotic dinosaurs that have attracted huge crowds to museums and other institutions throughout the country. Dinamation is the brainchild of a former airline pilot named Chris May, though he certainly did not invent the robotic dinosaur idea. Animated figures of one sort or another have been popular attractions for a long time, particularly in theme parks like those run by the Disney corporation. May's immediate inspiration came from a Japanese company that manufactured dinosaur robots for shopping centers and the like. He got together the money to buy the company's American marketing rights before starting out on his own. The first models his company marketed were fairly crude. He then enlisted the aid of a panel of high-powered scientific advisers, including Robert T. Bakker of the University of Colorado, one of the real pioneers of the new scientific view of dinosaurs. By 1986 Dinamation was producing much more realistic, and scientifically accurate, models. They were then rented to various institutions, and began pulling in record-breaking crowds. People, particularly kids, loved the creatures that moved their heads and tails, rolled their eyes, and roared and hissed.

Not all scientists have reacted enthusiastically to the robots. Large institutions like New York's American Museum of Natural History and the Field Museum in Chicago simply will not display the models, contending they are too speculative, and more suited for a theme park than a museum. Yet some of the larger institutions like the Smithsonian in Washington, D.C., and scores of smaller ones have welcomed the moving models as a wonderful way of educating as well as entertaining.

The controversy, which reflects two basically different philosophies about what a museum is supposed to do, is not likely to be resolved soon. So long as the robots draw the crowds, there are museums that will put them on display.

Dinamation caught the crest of rising interest in dinosaurs, and there is an undeniable novelty aspect to the exhibit. There are limits to the number of people who will continue to pay extra to see the same model dinosaurs doing the same thing. Dinamation is well aware of this and is planning for the future. A new set of robotic figures called "Real Sea Monsters: Dinosaurs of the Deep," featuring such fearsome giants as the long-necked *Elasmosaurus* and the toothy archaic whale *Basilosaurus*, began touring the country in 1989. Though the creatures are not as well known as dinosaurs, this exhibit has been drawing enthusiastic, and wide-eyed crowds. And there is more to come. Prehistoric mammals like the giant sloth have been added to the company's cast of robots. There are plans for "future zoo" models of animals that might evolve at some time in the future, and an elaborate Dry Aquarium featuring models of sea creatures that are difficult or impossible to exhibit in standard aquariums.

Besides the models, the company has begun a magazine devoted to dinosaurs, and has Dinosaur Valley Expeditions that give participants a "hands-on" tour of some of the great dinosaur fossil sites in the American West. There are also a host of other dinosaur-centered educational programs. Dinamation has no intention of fading away once interest in the dinosaur robots fades.

The company's California workshops are not open to visitors. Most Dinamation displays feature a good explanation of how the dinosaur or other models are created and how they work. You can, however, write the company for information on where exhibits are currently on display or for information on the expeditions or other activities.

Sequoia Creative, Inc.

Where: 9265 Borden Avenue, Sun Valley, CA 91352
Phone: (818) 768-4269

This company, founded by a couple of former Disney employees, has produced a wide variety of popular animated attractions, including some animated dinosaurs. Their most ambitious project has been the Kingdom of the Dinosaurs attraction at Knott's Berry Farm. The company also produced the animated King Kong that confronts visitors at the Universal City tour in Hollywood.

Kokoro

Where: Los Angeles office, 22900 Ventura Boulevard, Woodland Hills, CA 91364
Phone: (818) 992-8918

This Japanese company has been building robotic dinosaurs for over twenty years, and considers itself world leader in this field. The Kokoro robots have not toured the United States as widely as those of competitor Dinamation, but there have been major exhibitions, including a 1991 exhibit at the Philadelphia Academy of Sciences. The company also builds stationary models. There is a Kokoro *Tyrannosaurus* at the Lawrence Hall of Science in Berkeley, California, and a woolly mammoth at the George C. Page Museum at the La Brea Tar Pits in Los Angeles.

The Kokoro collection of robotic creatures includes, in addition to dinosaurs, marine and flying reptiles and extinct mammals such as saber-toothed cats, the giant flightless bird *Diatryma*, and a family of early human ancestors.

California Academy of Science

Where: Golden Gate Park, San Francisco, CA 94118-4599
Hours: Every day from 10:00 A.M.-5:00 P.M., with extended evening hours from July 4th through Labor Day.
Admission: Adults $4; Children 12 to 17 years and Seniors $2; Children 6 to 11 years $1; Children under 5 years free. The first Wednesday of every month is free.
Phone: (415) 750-7145

In June of 1990 the Academy opened a spectacular new exhibit, Life Through Time. It takes visitors through three billion years of evolution, beginning with an introductory video on the key concepts of evolution and geological time. Then, using reconstructed skeletons, fossils, models, videos, text, interactive computer programs, as well as living plants and animals, the exhibits portray the course of life on Earth. There are scenes of early life in the sea and on land. These exhibits of early life are not for the faint of heart. They contain such things as a foot-long cockroach, an automated eight-foot-long millipede, and a three-foot scorpion that rears up into a striking position.

After that the dinosaurs seem almost cuddly, though the centerpiece of the dinosaur display is life-size models of three *Deinonychus*, small agile, carnivorous dinosaurs. The trio appears frozen in a moment of time, running with claws outstretched toward the viewer.

The dinosaurs, as this exhibit clearly explains, never truly became extinct. One branch of dinosaurs evolved into birds. After the large ruling dinosaurs died out, the land was dominated for a time by descendants of the dinosaurs, large flightless birds, though these creatures rarely get much attention in museums. The Academy has a diorama showing two enor-

mous *Diatryma* (eight-foot-tall flightless birds) guarding their young from encroaching *Pachyaenas* (wolflike mammals). There are also scenes showing the development of larger mammals, such as rhinos, whales, and humans, and the changing world of the Ice Age.

Museum of Paleontology, University of California

Where: On the campus of the University of California, Berkeley. Mailing address, 7 Earth Sciences Building, Berkeley, CA 94720

Hours: Monday through Friday, 8:00 A.M.-5:00 P.M.; Saturday, 1:00 P.M.-5:00 P.M. Closed Thanksgiving, Christmas, and 4th of July.

Phone: (415) 642-3733 or (415) 642-1821

The main entrance to the museum is guarded by a fine bronze statue of *Smilodon*, largest and most famous of the saber-toothed cats. *Smilodon* remains were found in abundance in the La Brea Tar Pits, and it is the state fossil of California. Nearby is a skeleton of *Smilodon* from the Tar Pits, and a skeleton of the dire wolf, the most common mammal fossil found in the Tar Pits.

The best single dinosaur in the collection is an excellent cast of a spectacularly crested duck-billed dinosaur. There are also fossils of marine reptiles like the plesiosaurs and ichthyosaurs. On the second floor there is a large mural of marine carnivores from the Age of Dinosaurs.

Wheel Inn Restaurant

Where: On the north side of I-10 at Cabazon, CA.

Hours: Open 24 hours

Arguably the greatest roadside attraction in America are the two absolutely gigantic dinosaur models next to the Wheel Inn Restaurant in Cabazon, California, in the desert not far from Palm Springs. The dinosaurs are Dinny, a 150-foot-long steel-and-concrete *Brontosaurus*, and Rex, a 65-foot-high *Tyrannosaurus*. Both these models are far larger than the real things, which were quite gigantic enough. A set of steel stairs leads up Dinny's side to a small museum and gift shop in the monster's belly.

Both of these fantastic creatures were the creation of Claude Bell. He dreamed of such structures from the time he was a boy in Atlantic City and his uncle took him to see Lucy, a six-story building in the shape of an elephant. When asked why he built dinosaurs, Bell replied, "Because they're the biggest thing there is." He made them even bigger.

Construction of Dinny was begun in 1964 and took eleven years and cost $250,000. It was built of steel from a washed-out bridge and 1,200 sacks of surplus concrete.

The restaurant itself boasts of "Delicious home cooking— Famous homemade pies—Featuring Fresh Strawberry all year and our special Peanut Butter Cream Pie. Discount Art Show with over 500 paintings, gifts, turquoise jewelry, and a full selection of various tools at very low prices . . ."

This is a genuine American phenomenon. If you're in the vicinity, don't miss this place.

John Day Fossil Beds
National Monument

Where: Park headquarters is located in the city of John Day at 420
W. Main Street, John Day, OR 97845
Phone: (503) 987-2333

This region in eastern Oregon is named after pioneer trapper
and explorer John Day. Fossil bones, mostly those of prehistoric mammals, and other types of fossils have been found
here since the 1860s. The fossil beds contain a vast record of
the past from more than 50 million years ago to about 5 million
years ago. To protect the valuable natural and scientific resource, the John Day Fossil Beds National Monument was
created in 1974. Today it encompasses more than 14,030
acres, including the fossil beds and the surrounding semidesert
landscape. Points of interest in the park are well marked, but
widely scattered, so it is essential for the visitor to stop first at
the main park headquarters in the city of John Day for information on drives, trails, and museums, as well as the oppor-
tunities for fishing and wildlife observation. The headquarters
also has a display of representative fossils that have been found
within the park. A laboratory is nearby where, at times, a
technician can be seen preparing fossils for display. Some of
the most interesting fossils to be observed while walking
through the park are not those of animals, but those of plants.
The visitor can actually see an entire ancient tree limb embedded in a rock.

   At one time this area was a subtropical forest in which
alligators, rhinoceroses, and titanotheres flourished in the
warm, moist climate. Volcanoes also were common, period-

ically spewing forth cinders and ash. Heavy rains inundated the loose ash, producing mudflows which began the formation of the many types of fossils found today.

The Prehistoric Gardens

Where: 36848 Highway 101 South, Port Orford, OR 97465
              (midway between Port Orford and Gold Beach)
Hours: Every day from 8:00 A.M. until dusk.
Admission: Adults $4.50; Students 12 to 18 years and Seniors
              $3.50; Children 5 to 11 years $2.50; Children 4 years
              and under free.
Phone: (503) 332-4463

In protected valleys along the Oregon coast lush temperate zone rain forests have developed. There are gigantic ferns, mosses hanging from the tall trees, and skunk cabbages with huge tropical leaves. This is the sort of environment in which one imagines dinosaurs would have lived. And in one of these valleys sculptor and metal worker E. V. Nelson has been creating his own vision of the prehistoric world since 1953. As the visitor wanders through the winding trails deep in the shady forest of ferns and giant spruce, he or she will encounter life-size replicas of dinosaurs and other prehistoric creatures. These models are not of museum-quality accuracy, but some of them, like *Brachiosaurus*, are absolutely enormous, and lots of fun to see. This place is definitely a cut above the usual roadside dinosaur park. There is a gift and souvenir shop nearby featuring models, books, and other items with a prehistoric theme.

WASHINGTON

Pacific Science Center

Where: 200 Second Avenue North, Seattle, WA 98109
Hours: Monday through Friday, 10:00 A.M.-5:00 P.M.; Saturday and Sunday, 10:00 A.M.-6:00 P.M. Open later during the summer months.
Admission: Adults $4.50; Students and Seniors $3.50; Children 2 to 5 years $1.50
Phone: (206) 443-2001

The Pacific Science Center is home base for one of the most popular exhibits around, Dinosaurs: A Journey Through Time, which features five lifelike, moving and roaring dinosaur models.

It's important to note that this exhibit is not always at the Science Center. It travels widely, attracting record crowds wherever it goes. So before rushing off to Seattle, call to find out if the exhibit is there, and if not, where it is, and where it's going to be.

Stars of the exhibit are the full-size or half-size computerized models of five dinosaurs, *Tyrannosaurus rex*, *Pachycephalosaurus*, *Stegosaurus*, *Triceratops*, and *Apatosaurus*. They move their heads and tails, open their mouths, roll their eyes, and roar. We don't know whether dinosaurs really roared, but these certainly do. The very young may be frightened by the lifelike models, but most love them. The dinosaurs are surrounded by a limited, but fairly realistic, environment with bubbling mudpots and a waterfall.

There are some nonmoving parts of this exhibit as well, a full-sized cast of a *Memenchisaurus*, a dinosaur footprint, and a cutaway model leg of a *Tyrannosaurus*.

In addition, there are a variety of computer games and skeleton puzzles that will hold the attention of young visitors.

Alaska, Hawaii, and Canada

ALASKA

University of Alaska Museum

Where: 907 Yukon Drive, Fairbanks, AK 99775-1200
Hours: May and September, 9:00 A.M.-5:00 P.M.; June, July, and August, 9:00 A.M.-7:00 P.M.; October through April, noon-5:00 P.M. Closed Thanksgiving, Christmas, and New Year's Day.
Admission: Adults $3; Seniors, Military, and Students $2.50; Family of four $10; Children under 12 years free.
Phone: (907) 474-7505

Alaska may seem a very unlikely place to look for dinosaurs. And the display of dinosaur bones at the University of Alaska Museum is not very much to look at—a few small bones and fragments in glass cases. But if these fossils aren't much to see, they give the visitor a lot to think about, because they were found on Alaska's North Slope, well above the Arctic Circle. Most of the dinosaurs found on the North Shope were hadrosaurs or duck-billed dinosaurs, one of the most common and widespread groups of dinosaurs.

In the days of the dinosaurs the climate of the North Slope was nowhere near as cold as it is today, but it was certainly not the steamy tropical environment which we usually think of as the dinosaur's habitat. And it was dark. Then as now, the sun did not appear above the horizon for part of the long winter. That would certainly affect plant life and leave the plant-eating hadrosaurs little or no food. How did they survive? Perhaps during the winter they migrated thousands of miles to areas richer in vegetation. Whatever they did, the North Slope fossils are clear evidence that dinosaurs were tough creatures, with an ability to adapt to all sorts of hostile conditions.

That makes the mystery of their extinction more puzzling than ever.

It has long been known that large mammals like the woolly mammoth flourished in Alaska during the Ice Age. The museum has a formidable collection of bones from Ice Age mammals. Pride of the museum's collection is Blue Babe, a beautifully preserved specimen of the now-extinct Alaska steppe bison. The remains are so complete that scientists were able to determine that the creature was killed by an American lion, but the lion didn't eat much and the carcass was silted over and permanently frozen. The bluish color of the carcass is the result of a chemical reaction between the animal tissue, iron in the soil, and the air. The bison was nicknamed Blue Babe after the legend of Paul Bunyan and his giant blue ox.

The preserved partial remains of Effie, a young mammoth that died in the Fairbanks area some 21,000 years ago, are also on display. Effie is the best-preserved mammoth to be found in North America. Bones, tusks, and teeth are common finds throughout the far north, and some are on display in this museum. What is rare about Effie is the preservation of soft tissue such as skin and muscle.

The dinosaur and prehistoric mammal exhibits in this museum are not as visually impressive as exhibits in many larger museums, but Alaska is unique, and so are these exhibits.

Paradise Park

Where: 3737 Manoa Road, Honolulu, HI 96822
Hours: 9:30 A.M.-5:00 P.M. every day except Christmas.
Admission: Adults $13.95; Seniors $10.95; Children 7 to 12 years
               $8.95; Children 3 to 6 years $5.95, under 3 years free
Phone: (808) 988-2141

The dinosaurs had died out before the islands of Hawaii were ever formed. Therefore, there are no dinosaur fossils to be found there, and few fossils of any kind. But the visitor can still see dinosaurs at the popular Paradise Park attraction, which until recently had featured primarily colorful gardens and exotic birds. However, in 1991 the park opened a permanent exhibit of Dinamation's robotic dinosaurs. Many of these models, like the *Stegosaurus* and *Triceratops*, had been part of Dinamation's traveling exhibits. Amid the lush and colorful scenery of Manoa Valley they have found a permanent home.

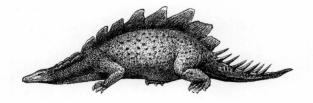

CANADA

Parrsboro, Nova Scotia

Where: From Halifax, Nova Scotia, take Highway 102 northwest
          to Truro, exit 14A, then Highway 2 west to Parrsboro. Write
          Nova Scotia Department of Tourism and Culture, P.O.
          Box 130, Halifax, Nova Scotia B31 2M7
Phone: (800) 341-6096

For years the little town of Parrsboro was best known to tourists because it was situated on the Bay of Fundy, the place that has the highest tides in the world. These tides exposed interesting rocks and fossils, and so the region sometimes attracted amateur geologists and fossil hunters. There was a regular Rockhound Roundup every August, but the region was not considered a major or significant fossil site. In the 1980s the Parrsboro area lost its amateur status after scientists announced the discovery of thousands of pieces of fossilized bone dating from the time between the Triassic and Jurassic periods, about 230 million years ago. Scientists are extremely interested in this time period, for dinosaurs were first beginning to emerge and so were the tritheledonts, reptiles most closely related to mammals. It also appears to have been a period of mass extinction. Over 40 percent of the known species died off between the Triassic and Jurassic periods, an even more dramatic mass death than occurred 65 million years ago when the dinosaurs died off.

Most of the fossils are fragmented, tiny and frankly not much to look at, but for understanding the history of life on earth they are very significant. Tritheledonts had never been found in North America before, and fossils were extremely rare anywhere. This was the largest discovery of these rare and important fossils in the world. A local fossil collector found what may be the world's smallest dinosaur footprints. The three-toed, half-inch-long prints were made by a creature no larger than a robin. And there was lots more.

The theory that the extinction of the dinosaurs was caused by the collision of Earth with an asteroid, which disrupted the world's climate, has been widely discussed. One problem with the theory is that no one has been able to find the spot where this collision took place. But in Quebec there is a huge impact crater called the Manicouagan crater that was formed at about the time of the extinctions at the end of the Triassic. The size of the crater suggests that the asteroid that hit the Earth must have been six miles wide and weighed four million tons. It is far from certain that the impact that created this crater also caused the extinctions, but the possibility is an exciting one and focused a lot of scientific and other attention on the Parrsboro discoveries. Said one scientist: "The find is like a Rosetta stone. This period was one of tremendous geological upheaval. The continents were beginning to split apart, and there was a turnover among the animals. The modern world was basically set during this time."

News of the discoveries got a tremendous amount of publicity, and brought a flood of tourists to the region, and with them came problems. Since the fossil sites are extremely fragile, stringent measures had to be enacted to protect them. The old freewheeling days of fossil collecting were over.

The government is planning to build a major museum in the area, but at present there are displays of the fossils at the Parrsboro Geological Mineral and Gem Museum and the Parrsboro Rock and Mineral Shop. At the shop Eldon George will show you the world's smallest dinosaur footprint that he discovered in 1984. The footprint, on a piece of red sandstone, fits nicely under a penny. Visitors can also buy shirts and caps touting Parrsboro as "The Dinosaur Capital of the World" and "Home of the World's Smallest Dinosaur."

There's lots more to see in the region, including the famous Bay of Fundy tides. A word of warning: these tides are not only the highest in the world, they come in with astonishing speed. Be sure to check the time tides come in before doing any exploring near the water.

Nova Scotia Museum

Where: 1747 Summer Street, Halifax, Nova Scotia B3H 3A6
Hours: Summer: Monday through Saturday, 9:30 A.M.-5:30
               P.M.; Sunday, 1:00 P.M.-5:30 P.M. Open Wednesday
               until 8:00 P.M. Closed Monday and one-half hour ear-
               lier during the winter.
Admission: Donations accepted
Phone: (902) 429-4610

This museum has a modest display of fossils. Significantly, however, it has some of the celebrated discoveries from Parrs-boro. Many of these discoveries were made by scientists from the United States and they were shipped off to Harvard and Columbia for further study. This created quite a stir in Canada's House of Commons. Canadian pride was offended. There were even charges of a "Fossilgate." But it turned out that the fossils were only on loan because small institutions like the Nova Scotia Museum simply didn't have the expertise for proper identification and research. But now they do have some of the original fossils back.

Redpath Museum

Where: 859 Sherbrooke Street West, Montreal, Quebec, Canada
H3A 2K6
Hours: Monday through Friday 9:00 A.M.-5:00 P.M.
Phone: (514) 398-4092

This is a museum to be seen more for the way its exhibits are displayed than for the exhibits themselves. Redpath is a very old museum, built in 1882 to house the collections of McGill University. It is the first specially designed museum building in Canada. It is now primarily a teaching and research museum, and little attempt has been made to modernize the displays to suit the taste of today's visitors. The collection is eccentric, reflecting nineteenth-century tastes in artifact acquisition: everything from a shrunken head to a large collection of poisonous fishes. There are some nice marine reptile fossils in the front gallery. The prize of the fossil collection is part of *Hylonomus lyelli*, the oldest-known reptile.

Royal Ontario Museum

Where: 100 Queen's Park, Toronto, Ontario, Canada M5S
2C6
Hours: Tuesday through Sunday, 10:00 A.M.-6:00 P.M.; open until 8:00 P.M. Tuesday and Thursday. Closed Monday except during the summer months.
Admission: Adults $6; Seniors, Students, and Children $3.25; Families $13.
Phone: (416) 586-5549

Canada's largest museum, and one of the largest in North America, has a celebrated collection of ancient Chinese ar-

tifacts, a world-famous collection of textiles and, of course, dinosaurs. There are thirteen full dinosaur skeletons, and partial skeletons of many more species on display in the Dinosaur Gallery, located on the second floor of the main Royal Ontario Museum building. The museum has a particularly fine collection of hadrosaurs, commonly called duck-billed dinosaurs. One of the most prized skeletons is the crested hadrosaur *Parasaurolophus*, still displayed in the same sandstone block in which it was found. On the other hand, the menacing-looking *Albertosaurus* leans out over the aisle, and appears ready to attack a horned dinosaur and a couple of hadrosaurs.

Faint strains of eerie music greet visitors to the section of

the Dinosaur Gallery that contains fossils from the Jurassic period. Here a couple of carnivorous *Allosaurus* challenge a *Stegosaurus* and a *Camptosaurus*. Throughout the displays there are video terminals that show what the bones would have looked like with flesh on them, and discuss dinosaur feeding habits, movement, and posture.

Elsewhere, skeletons are set in a life-size diorama to show a saber-toothed cat, a Harlan's ground sloth, and other ancient mammals struggling in the Rancho La Brea Tar Pits. A 70-million-year-old underwater scene is inhabited by mosasaurs and a plesiosaur, marine reptiles from the Age of Dinosaurs. There is also a special display of human evolution.

Canadian Museum of Nature

Where: Metcalfe and McLeod Streets, in downtown Ottawa. Mailing address, P.O. Box 3443, Station "D," Ottawa, Ontario, Canada K1P 6P4

Hours: May 1 to Labor Day, 9:30 A.M.-5:00 P.M.; after Labor Day to April 30, daily 10:00 A.M.-5:00 P.M., Thursday until 8:00 P.M.

Admission: Adults $2; Seniors and Students $1.50; Children 6 to 16 years $1; Children under 6 years free; Family $5. Free on Thursday.

Phone: (613) 990-7582

Formerly called the National Museum of Natural Sciences, this institution is impressive and historic on the outside, and newly refurbished on the inside. In recent years there have been a lot of major dinosaur discoveries in western Canada, and Canadians take great pride in them. All of the dozen or so dinosaurs on display in this excellent collection come from western Canada. Some, like *Triceratops* and the duck-billed dinosaurs, are familiar to anyone with even a smattering of dinosaurian knowledge. Others, like *Stenonychosaurus*, considered to be one of the most intelligent dinosaurs, are not often seen in museums. The visitor can touch a cast of fossil dinosaur skin, and a real fossil dinosaur bone.

The dinosaur exhibit is part of the Life Through the Ages Hall, which covers two floors of the museum and begins with a brief film on the origin of life on Earth. On the second floor are the fossils of the contemporaries of the dinosaurs, particularly the marine reptiles. Throughout the Age of Dinosaurs a large part of Canada was underwater. There is another brief film about the still mysterious extinction of the dinosaurs, and that leads visitors to the exhibit of fossil mammals. Here there are mastodons, mammoths, saber-toothed cats, and giant beavers. What happened to all of these animals, which lived throughout North America as recently as ten thousand years ago? That is a mystery nearly as great as the extinction of the dinosaurs, and it is explored in the exhibit.

Tyrrell Museum of Palaeontology

Where: On the north side of the Red Deer River, four miles
northwest of Drumheller, Alberta, Canada, on Highway 838. Drumheller is 90 miles northeast of Calgary,
and 180 miles south of Edmonton. Mailing address,
Box 7500, Drumheller, Alberta, Canada T0J 0Y0

Hours: Summer: Victoria Day weekend to Thanksgiving Day,
9:00 A.M.-9:00 P.M. Winter: After Thanksgiving Day to
Victoria Day weekend 10:00 A.M.-5:00 P.M. Tuesday
through Sunday. Closed Monday except for public holidays. Also closed on Christmas Day.

Admission: There is no regular admission, but donations are wel-
come, encouraged, and deserved.

Phone: (403) 823-7707

It might seem foolish to open a $20-million, world-class mu-
seum in what a lot of people would regard as the middle of
nowhere. It takes over an hour to drive to the Tyrrell from
Calgary, and over three hours from Edmonton. And neither
of these cities are really major metropolitan areas. Visitors who
want to see this museum really have to make an effort. But
the effort is more than worthwhile. The museum, opened in
1985, has one of the largest and most up-to-date dinosaur
displays anywhere. The exhibit easily matches those in large
metropolitan museums, and surpasses most of them.

While the Tyrrell is not near any major population center,
it is very near some of the richest dinosaur fossil quarries in
the world. It is meant to serve not only as a wonderful experience for dinosaur-loving tourists, but as a major research
center for scientists. The paleontological riches of the region
were first uncovered by geographer/geologist Joseph Burr Tyrrell, for whom the museum was named, in 1884. There was
a burst of excavation in the area around the turn of the century.

Work picked up again as interest in dinosaurs rose in the 1970s. It was then that the Province of Alberta decided to build the new facility near the little town of Drumheller.

A tour of the museum begins with exhibits on the history of the Earth and early life. But it is the Dinosaur Hall that everyone wants to see. There are thirty-five full dinosaur skeletons on display, and the partial remains of at least 150 more, the largest number of dinosaur fossils assembled under one roof anywhere. Most of these fossils were found in Alberta. The displays of such species as *Maiasaura*, *Hypacrosaurus*, and *Albertosaurus* are both dramatic and dynamic. There are also fully fleshed-out reconstructions and murals in the same postures as the skeletons. In addition, there is a Marine Gallery which features the fossils of such marine reptiles as the plesiosaur.

The Hall of the Age of Mammals has unusual specimens, like the lumbering *Uintatherium*, and the more familiar saber-toothed cats and giant bison.

Through a large glass window in the Preparation Laboratory, visitors can look in at scientists and technicians at the painstaking task of cleaning and assembling fossils. Next to Dinosaur Hall the visitor can stroll through the Palaeoconservatory, a light and airy greenhouse that is home to over a hundred living descendants of plants that grew 350 to 15 million years ago. A trip through the museum takes anywhere from two to three hours.

The museum is located in Midland Provincial Park and, after a visit with the dinosaurs, visitors can stroll along well-marked paths to explore the bleakly, beautiful Badlands landscape.

Tyrrell Museum Field Station

Where: In Dinosaur Provincial Park, approximately 30 miles north of Brooks, Alberta. Mailing address, Box 60, Patricia, Alberta, Canada T0J 2K0

Hours: Summer: Victoria Day weekend to Labor Day, 9:00 A.M.-9:00 P.M. Winter: Wednesday through Sunday, 10:00 A.M.-5:00 P.M. Closed Monday, Tuesday, and Christmas Day

Admission: Donations are welcomed and encouraged.

Phone: (403) 378-4342

In 1955 thousands of acres of the Badlands of south-central Alberta, where some of the richest deposits of dinosaur fossils are located, were set aside as Dinosaur Provincial Park. This was primarily to protect the bones from zealous amateurs and would-be fossil entrepreneurs. In 1979 the United Nations Educational, Scientific, and Cultural Organization (UNESCO) named it a World Heritage Site, ranking it right up there with such geographical and cultural treasures as the Grand Canyon, the Acropolis, and the pyramids of Egypt. Remains of thirty-five different species of dinosaur have been found in the park. The scenery was and is spectacular, but the casual visitor isn't allowed to go fossil hunting. In 1987 the Tyrrell Museum opened its Field Station in the park. The station is a center for research, and a place where visitors can learn about the fossils found in the park.

There are fossil displays and a variety of programs and special events for visitors. There is also a viewing window for visitors to watch technicians prepare fossils brought in from the field.

Drumheller Dinosaur Country

Where: Write to Big Country Tourist Association, P.O. Box 2308, Drumheller, Alberta, Canada T0J 0Y0

Phone: (403) 823-5885

The big attraction at the town of Drumheller is the Tyrrell Museum of Palaeontology. But local businesses have capitalized on the dinosaur theme with a variety of rock and fossil shops and a great big (though not terribly accurate) model of *Tyrannosaurus rex* which stands at the bridge over the Red Deer River. It's a favorite spot for family photos. Visitors can spend the night at the Dinosaur Hotel or the Dinosaur Motel, camp out at the Dinosaur Trail Campground or the Dinosaur Trailer Court, and for the sportsman there is the Dinosaur Trail Golf & Country Club. There actually is a Dinosaur Trail, a thirty-mile circular route beginning and ending in Drumheller. It's a scenic drive that provides spectacular views of the Badlands and other points of interest, including a crossing of the Red Deer River on one of the last remaining cable ferries in Alberta. Since a visit to the Tyrrell and/or the Field Station will probably require an overnight stay, Drumheller is probably the place to stay.

Calgary Zoo and
Prehistoric Park

Where: Mailing address, P.O. Box 3036, Station "B," Calgary,
             Alberta, Canada T2M 4R8
Hours: Gates at the Zoo and Prehistoric Park are open at 9:00
             A.M. Closing hours are adjusted seasonally. The Pre-
             historic Park itself is open from mid-May until mid-
             November, weather permitting.
Admission: Adults $6.50; Seniors, $4; Children 12 to 17 years $4;
             Children 2 to 11 years $3; Children under 2 years free.
Phone: (403) 232-9372

Dinosaurs are as popular an attraction at the Calgary Zoo as gorillas and tigers. Perhaps even more popular. Attached to the zoo is a 6.5-acre park that is set up to look like western Canada might have looked during the Age of Dinosaurs. There are plants that would have grown in the ancient world, hand-sculpted rocks that simulate volcanoes or newly emergent mountains. Most of all, there are full-scale and very lifelike models of dinosaurs and other animals from that era, strate-gically placed along the path. At one turn there is a *Tyran-nosaurus*; half-hidden in the vegetation is the armored *Ankylosaurus*; towering above the visitor is the gigantic *Bron-tosaurus* or *Apatosaurus*. A long-necked *Elasmosaurus* sticks its head out of the water, and a *Pteranodon* appears to soar above the trail. All-in-all, there are some thirty of these re-plicas, most extremely well done. This is one of the best ex-hibits of its type, and a wonderful place to take pictures, or just wander around and contemplate what it would be like if those things were really alive!

Saskatchewan Museum of Natural History

Where: College and Albert streets, Regina, Saskatchewan, Canada
S4P 3V7
Hours: From May 1 to Labor Day, 9:00 A.M.-8:30 P.M.; after Labor
Day to April 30, 9:00 A.M.-4:30 P.M.
Phone: (306) 787-2815

Megamunch is the big favorite here. She's a robotic *Tyran-nosaurus*, Canada's first. Children all over the province chipped in to purchase the robot, and they selected her name.

In the museum's excellent new Earth Sciences Gallery the visitor walks past dioramas and other displays that clearly and beautifully illustrate Saskatchewan's evolution through two billion years of geological history. For a large part of this time much of the province was under the sea, and one of the most impressive displays shows the marine reptiles *Mososaurus* and *Elasmosaurus*.

A dinosaur diorama shows *Tyrannosaurus* hiding in the vegetation getting ready to attack *Edmontosaurus*, a flat-headed, duck-billed dinosaur. During the last days of the Age of Dinosaurs huge herds of horned dinosaurs, particularly the well-known *Triceratops*, roamed what is now Canada, and fossils and models of this creature are well represented in the collection.

Generally, in museums it is the dinosaurs that get all the attention. This museum, however, has a not-to-be-overlooked exhibit of fossils, models, and paintings of prehistoric Canadian mammals, from mastodons and the gigantic rhinoceros-like brontotheres, giant pigs and giant bisons, to tiny horses and bone-crushing dogs. There is even a nice display of prehistoric prairie dogs.

Photograph Credits

Academy of Natural Sciences, Philadelphia. Copyright 1987 Harvey A. Duze, 1; Photo by David Bennett, 32

American Museum of Natural History, New York City. Courtesy Department Library Services, Photo by D. Finnin, 5

Aurora Historical Museum, Aurora, IL, 88

Behringer-Crawford Museum, Covington, KY. Courtesy of Greg Harper, 73

California Academy of Science, San Francisco. Susan Middleton C.A.S. © 1990, 176

Carter County Museum, Ekalaka, MT, 158

The Children's Museum, Indianapolis, IN, 83

Cleveland Museum of Natural History, Cleveland, OH, 76

© 1988 Dinamation International Corp. Photo by Lydia Cutter, 173

Dinosaur National Park, 137

Dinosaur Park, Rapid City, SD, 149

The DinoStore, Birmingham, AL, 63

Copyright 1990 The Walt Disney Company, 39, 58

Field Museum of Natural History, Chicago, 85

Jim Gary, 27

Ghost Ranch, Abiquiu, NM, 123

Dean Hannotte, 7

Bonnie Heppard, Kenton, OK, 107

Houston Museum of Natural Science. Marketing and Communications Department, 111

Bud Jones Taxidermy, 56

Knott's Berry Farm, 168

The Mammoth Site, Hot Springs, SD. Photo by Paul Horsted, 129

Mill Canyon Dinosaur Site, 143

Missouri Department of Natural Resources, Mastodon State Park, Imperial, MO, 97

National Museum of Natural History, Smithsonian Institution, 42

New Mexico Museum of Natural History. David A. Thomas, sculptor, 111

North Carolina Maritime Museum, Beaufort, NC. Scott Taylor Fossil Exhibit, 52

North Carolina State Museum of Natural Sciences, Raleigh, NC, 51

The Ohio Historical Center, Columbus, OH, 78

Pacific Science Center, Seattle, WA, 161

Index

Academy of Natural Sciences,
  The, *xiii*, 31–33, 174
Agate Fossil Beds National Monu-
  ment, 104–5
Alabama, 61–64
Alaska, 185–86
Albertosaurus, 84, 120, 193, 198
Allosaurus, 30, 164
  bones, 137, 139
  models, 57, 145, 163
  skeletons, 11, 36, 60, 89, 103,
    113, 114, 139, 141, 194
American Museum of Natural His-
  tory, *xiii*, 3–6, 9, 109, 122,
  171
Anatosaurus, 20, 89, 158
Ankylosaurs, 100
Ankylosaurus, 201
Anniston Museum of Natural His-
  tory, 64
Apatosaurus. See Brontosaurus
Archaeopteryx, 51, 65, 67
Arizona, 125–27
Arizona Museum of Science and
  Technology, 127
Arkansas, 70
Asteroid crater, 189
Audubon Zoo, 65
Aurora Fossil Museum, 50
Aurora Historical Museum, 88

Baluchitherium, 102
Barosaurus, 4, 141
Basilosaurus, 43, 61–62
Beavers, giant, 77, 82, 89, 102,
  195
Behringer-Crawford Museum, 81
Big Bend National Park, 115–16
Big Bone Lick State Park, 79–80

Bisons, giant, 77, 80, 101, 117,
  186, 198, 202
bones, 69, 100, 159
Blue Licks Battlefield State Park,
  80–81
Brachiosaurus, 120, 131, 132, 180
Brazosport Museum of Natural
  Science, 113
Brontosaurus, *xii*, 3, 8, 10, 117,
  155
bones, 36, 89, 118, 137, 145
footprints, 114
models, 28, 57, 110, 124, 149,
  153, 177–78, 181, 201
skeletons, 18–20, 37, 84, 148
Brontotheres, 202
Buffalo Museum of Science, 11

Calgary Zoo and Prehistoric Park,
  201
California, *xii*, 163–78
California Academy of Science,
  175–76
Calvert Marine Museum, 44–45
Camarasaurus, 119, 131, 137, 138
Camptosaurus, 20, 137, 141, 164,
  194
Canada, *xi*, 10, 188–202
Canadian Museum of Nature,
  194–95
Carnegie Museum of Natural His-
  tory, The, *xiii*, 36–37, 104
Carter County Museum, 158
Children's Museum of Indianapo-
  lis, The, 83
Children's Museum of Maine,
  The, 23
Cincinnati Museum of Natural
  History, 77
Clayton Lake State Park, 124

Cleveland-Lloyd Dinosaur Quarry, 139
Cleveland Museum of National History, 75–76
Coelophysis, 15, 65, 120, 122
Colorado, 131–35
Connecticut, 18–22
Cope, Edward Drinker, 18, 35, 36, 104, 132–33

Dallas Museum of Natural History, 111–12
Day, John, Fossil Beds National Monument, 179–80
Deinonychus, 20, 31, 175
Denver Museum of Natural History, 134
Dilophasaurus, 22
Dimetrodon, 13, 116, 145
Dinamation, 171–72, 174, 187
Dino Productions, 134–35
Dinosaur Bone Cabin, 146
Dinosaur Hill, 133
Dinosaur Land, 48
Dinosaur National Monument, 136–37
Dinosaur Park, xii, 149–50
Dinosaur Quarries, 118
Dinosaur State Park, 21–22
Dinosaur Valley, 131
Dinosaur Valley State Park, 109–10
DinoStore, The, xi, 62–64
Diplodocus, 138
  bones, 116, 132, 138
  skeletons, 36–37, 41, 110
Dire wolves, 16, 165, 166, 177
Drumheller Dinosaur Country, 200
Dunn-Seiler Geological Museum, The, 68

Earth Sciences Museum, 142
Edmontosaurus, 92, 150, 202

Eggs, dinosaur, 23, 94, 142, 148, 156–57
Elasmosaurus, 31, 201, 202
Emery County Museum, 141
Exhibit Museum, 89

Fairbanks Museum and Planetarium, 25
Field Museum of Natural History, 84–86, 171
Flintstones Bedrock City, xii, 152
Florida, 57–60
Fort Worth Museum of Science and History, 112–13
Fryxell Geology Museum, The, 87

Garden Park Fossil Area, 132–33
Gary's, Jim, Twentieth-Century Dinosaurs, 26–29
Geology Museum, University of Wisconsin-Madison, 92
Georgia, 55–56
Glyptodon, 54, 72, 92, 116

Hadrosaurs, 26, 100, 177, 185–86, 193, 195
Hadrosaurus, 33
Hall, Leonard, Museum, 155
Hall, Ruth, Museum of Paleontology, 122–24
Hannotte, Dean, 7–8
Hawaii, 187
Houston Museum of Natural Science, 110
Hypacrosaurus, 198

Ichthyosaurs, 64, 99, 177
Idaho, 159
Idaho Museum of Natural History, 159
Iguanodon, 132
Illinois, 84–88
Indiana, 82–83
Iowa, 95

Jonas, Louis Paul, Studios, Inc., 9–10
Jones, Bud, Taxidermy, 56

Kansas, *xii*, 99–101
Kentucky, 79–81
Knight, Charles R., 85–86
Knott's Berry Farm, 167–69, 174
Kokoro, 174
Kritosaurus, 16

La Brea Tar Pits, *xiii*, 100, 110, 164–66, 174, 177
Lambeosaurus, 84
Land of Kong Dinosaur Park, 70
Louisiana, 65–67
LSU Museum of Geoscience, 66
Lucy, human ancestor, 11, 76, 90

McClung, Frank H., Museum, 72
Maiasaura, 148, 156–57, 198
Maine, 23–24
Maine State Museum, 24
Mammoths, 25, 37, 84, 87, 114, 117, 166
  bones, 24, 100, 101, 102, 112, 116, 151–52, 186, 195
  models, 48, 167
  skeletons, 16, 106, 141–42
Mammoth Site, The, 151–52
Marsh, Othniel Charles, 18–20, 104, 132–33
Maryland, 44–45
Massachusetts, 12–17
Mastodons, 25, 37, 84, 91–92, 202
  bones, 24, 26, 78, 81, 88, 89, 90, 92, 100, 101, 102, 116, 195
  models, 9, 53, 54, 80, 96–97
  skeletons, 13–14, 16, 29, 67, 71, 76, 82, 83
Mastodon State Park, 96–97
Memphis Pink Palace Museum, 71
Michigan, 89–90

Mill Canyon Dinosaur Trail, 143
Milwaukee Public Museum, 91–92
Minnesota, 94
Mississippi, 68–69
Mississippi Museum of Natural Science, 69
Missouri, 96–98
Montana, 156–58
Moore, Joseph, Museum, 82
Morrill Hall, 102–3
Morris Museum, The, 30
Mosasaurs, 11, 43, 87, 99, 102, 116, 150
  bones, 71, 112
  skeletons, 61, 92
Mososaurus, 202
Museum of Arts and Sciences, The, 55
Museum of Comparative Zoology, The, *xi*, 12–14
Museum of Geology, 150
Museum of Natural History, 99–100
Museum of Natural Science, The, 67
Museum of Northern Arizona, 126–27
Museum of Paleontology, University of California, 177
Museum of Science, 14
Museum of Science and History, 60
Museum of Texas Tech University, 114
Museum of the Chicago Academy of Sciences, The, 86
Museum of the Rockies, 156–57

Nash Dinosaurland, 16–17
National Museum of Natural History, Smithsonian Institution, 41–43, 171
Natural History Museum of Los Angeles County, 163–64

Nebraska, 102–6
New Jersey, 26–30
New Jersey State Museum, 26
New Mexico, 119–24
New Mexico Museum of Natural History, 119–20
New York, 3–11
New York State Museum, The, 8–9
North Carolina, 50–53
North Carolina Maritime Museum, 52–53
North Carolina Museum of Life and Science, 53
North Carolina State Museum of Natural Sciences, 50–51
North Dakota, 155
Nova Scotia Museum, 190

Ohio, 75–78
Ohio Historical Center, 78
Oklahoma, 117–18
Oklahoma Museum of Natural History, 117–18
O'Laurie, Dan, Museum, 144
Oregon, 179–80
Ornithomimus, 58
Orodromeus, 157

Pachycephalosaurus, 91, 158, 181
Pacific Science Center, 181
Page, George C., Museum of La Brea Discoveries, 164–66, 174
Paradise Park, 187
Parrsboro, Nova Scotia, xiii, 188–90
Peabody Museum, The, 18–20
Pennsylvania, 31–37
Pentaceratops sternbergii, 120
Petrified Forest National Park, 125–26
Plesiosaurs, 99, 102, 150, 177, 198
Plesiosaurus, 25

Pratt Museum of Natural History, 15–16
Prehistoric Gardens, The, 180
Prehistoric Journeys, xi, 169
Princeton Natural History Museum, 29–30
Pteranodon
    models, 30, 64, 98, 167, 201
    skeletons, 33, 99
Pterodactyls, 124
Pterosaurs, 11, 37, 102, 116

Quetzalcoatlus, 115–16, 119, 157

Rabbit Valley Quarry, 131–32
Red Mountain Museum, 61–62
Redpath Museum, 191
Rhinoceroses, 101, 102, 104, 118, 176
Riggs Hill, 132
Rowley, Robert, 140
Royal Ontario Museum, 191–94
Rutgers Geology Museum, 29

Saber-toothed cats, 37, 84, 110, 117, 150, 164, 165, 198
    bones, 51, 72, 195
    models, 167
    skeletons, 16, 68, 76
St. Louis Science Center, 98
San Diego Natural History Museum, 163
Saskatchewan Museum of Natural History, 202
Science Museum of Minnesota, The, 94
Sequoia Creative, Inc., 174
Sinclair Oil Company, 8, 10, 62–63
Skullduggery, 170
Sloths, giant ground, 49, 61, 77, 84, 95, 101, 102, 117, 166
Smilodon, 117, 177
South Carolina, 10, 54
South Carolina State Museum, 54

South Dakota, *xiii*, 149–53
Springfield Science Museum, 15
Stegosaurus
    bones, *xiv*, 3, 41, 137, 138
    models, 30, 57, 90, 119, 181, 187
    skeletons, 15, 20, 23, 36, 89, 103, 139, 141, 194
Stenonychosaurus, 195
Sternberg Memorial Museum, The, 100–101
Supersaurus, 142

Tennessee, 71–72
Tenontosaurus, 112–13
Texas, 109–16
Texas Memorial Museum, 116
Thomas, David A., 120–21
Titanotheres, 92, 150, 179
Tracks, dinosaur, 15–17, 21–22, 29, 30, 46, 47, 71, 72, 90, 109–10, 118, 124, 127, 139–40, 144, 181, 189
Trailside Museum, 105–6
Triceratops, 11, 91, 155, 195
    models, 41, 47, 98, 124, 138, 157, 181, 187, 202
    skulls, *xi*, 13, 16, 51, 68, 87, 127, 148, 155, 158
Tritheledonts, 188
Tyrannosaurus rex, *xiv*, 91, 202
    bones, 6, 41, 89
    models, 14, 15, 28, 48, 60, 83, 98, 110, 124, 138, 146–48, 167, 177–78, 181, 200, 201, 202
    skeletons, 3, 31–33, 37, 157
    skulls, 16, 20, 51, 87, 94, 114, 127, 150, 164
Tyrrell Museum Field Station, 199
Tyrrell Museum of Palaeontology, 196–98

Uintatherium, 198
Ultrasaurus, 33, 142
Universal Studios of Florida, 59–60
University of Alaska Museum, 185–86
University of Iowa Museum of Natural History, 95
University of Wyoming Geological Museum, 146–48
Utah, 136–45
Utah Field House of Natural History and Dinosaur Gardens, 138
Utah Museum of Natural History, 141–42

Vermont, 25
Vines, Robert A., Environmental Science Center, 113–14
Virginia, 46–48
Virginia Living Museum, 46
Virginia Museum of Natural History, 47

Wagner Free Institute of Science, *xiii*, 34–36
Wall Drug Dinosaur, 153–54
Walt Disney World, 57–58, 60
Warner Valley Dinosaur Tracksite, 144
Washington, state of, 181
Washington, DC, 41–43
Weber State College Museum of Natural Science, 145
West Virginia, 49
West Virginia Geological and Economic Survey, 49
Wheel Inn Restaurant, *xi*, 177–78
Wisconsin, *xiii*, 91–92
Wyoming, 146

Zygorhiza, 55, 69

Daniel Cohen has been a dinosaur nut since birth. **Susan Cohen** realized that she would either have to share this passion, or get a divorce. She has now developed a true enthusiasm for the "animals of extinction."

This book has given them an opportunity to "dig up" more dinosaur and other prehistoric exhibits, quarries, parks, stores, and other attractions than have ever been covered in any other volume. All the well-known places are here, of course. "But the great thrill," says Susan, "was finding places practically no one else had ever heard of.

"We found one fine museum that was so obscure that the police in a station located directly across the street didn't even know it was there," she adds.

The Cohens have written other books together, but this is their most ambitious joint project. "It was a lot of work, a lot of fun and we survived," says Daniel.